3X: Volume 2

By

Jermar Jerome Smith

PROLOGUE

Descending forward in this entertaining spectacle held outside that climbs a number of people in attendance and in show under the blazing hot summer sun. Entering amongst goes a figure not that very big in stature but what he lacks in height he makes up in his captivation in point of view to the overwhelming scenery. Where a ongoing contest involving thirty foot basketball jump shot making is the scenario displayed for any and all to join. But only if the host and hostess deem to be a proper wager by the open crowd fixated by the intrigued odds as to gaining a big promised prize.

Lavished and orchestrated in a amusement, carnival, and park gathering display. The overall gaming blueprint is arranged with of course a regulation ten foot ball hoop before an equipped outdoor court center that stretches in the ordinary feet with all its perimeters surrounding. Only this area which clears about twenty-five feet and nothing above is strictly housed to the hostess who's a very attractive young lady in a form fitting referee outfit that's taste to a feminine touch as her shorts raise beyond her smooth caramel thick packing thighs. That bounds the majority of young male population and excites them to engage into the chance opportune for stunt purposes mostly as she roles in the bid collecting from them. Accompanying at her side is the man who sends out the ball to the audience of the lucky individual looking to making their attempt a winning one instead of just another punk that loss out on another dollar. While also shouting from his bullhorn on which amount each sucka, excuse me contestant is willing to dish sold to the bet.

- Come on ya'll shoot to win. I know you got it. A make gets you a prize, a miss is twenty five. Who wanna try they luck ? Get a prize for you or your girl, come on ya'll stop being scared.

He calls to faithfully in sermon...

VIOLATORS

Slide open goes a drawer by a sudden hand. Retrieved comes a heavy satchel case prepped on to a desk. Upon a key to open, the person takes strict measures in handling the unidentified object. Inside buried into a foam hollow mold for holding. It's medium in size, appears electronic, and slightly resembles a vintage toaster but more compacted in size. There's a single slide switch by it's opening and a solid matte black coloring that shields it all around.

The creation is one of many by Merrill Malenko who devotes his spare time as a specialist salesman into crafting gadgets that are gateway to identifying almost anything. Whether physical or to some notes unseen although there. Having doing critical and sleepless research in the earlier months until now Malenko became curious to the everyday essential we as people all possess that which gives us life. Hence air, after reading he discovered multiples things in regards to the fruit of being and became obsessed with it drawing ideas for creations to manipulate it and eventually to his most passionate desire is to actually seeing air and having the ability to recognize any poisons, toxins, or parasites that it may contain.

It was a month and half ago that his very dream came into reality when he finished the last stages of this oxygen monitor dubbing it by name as a "Invisualator". The way of it working goes as he tests it as he hits the device's side switch before wrapping protective goggles on his eyes and it flicks off the light as the thick green laser beam catch a patch of the office's atmosphere and he observes the air with his own two, while gracing a smile in achieving the objective. A tap on the machine he does then in the same glow reveals the parasites infused. So proud of his work, Merrill even offered to lend his idea to a few possible investors that could be interested in the inception and put it to whatever use while compensating him to a hefty sum at his own asking. A natural business deal successful and then approved.

Entering his office before the darkness snagging a minor glimpse to the green glow is his Merrill's co-worker Porter. Off he shuts the light, while on comes his office's Porter feels free to shut on to view on his visit carrying mail.

- You keep on with that thing and your gonna X ray vision through your fucking brain.

- I'll just make a machine to reverse the effects if it comes to that.

- Same ol' Merrill, what you meddling on your latest creation this time. Twerking some of the bugs for that big sale soon.

- Nah it's perfect, I'm just joy testing for now. And what do I owe this pleasure to your interruption while I'm conducting business.

- Mail day !

- Anything good ? Let's see.

Porter gives off the mail as Merrill surfs through in careful eyes then eases over to his device with friendly hands, touching it over that even though it escapes Merrill sights not his senses that in a must he reminds for him to yield.

- Ah, ah ! Respect !

And he does lifting his hands off. In his skimming Merrill catches eyes to an envelope most unusual in the color solid blue that although strange just some how he can't resist in unwrapping. The note inside he reads in hurry excitement over each word with Porter peeping in noisy curiosity and asking could be gracing good news. Perhaps a seller for his gadget. Grinning raising the letter down by his side still in his hands he says.

- In fact it was.

- You...you serious.

- According to this letter and everything it's saying, nope damn serious.

- No shit...looks like inspector gadget's ass is finally going get his own show after all. Let me see ! What does it says ?

- It' a invitation by some foreign investors by the name of TIVOTU Nationalist. They're inviting me to a one time interview with my "Invisualator". If approved I look to net on contractual obligations a sum of fifteen million dollars upon signing.

The news is enough to shoot up congratulation spirits in shower from Porter.

- Congrats man, did it say the location.

- Further pass Fredericksburg. 1612 Desert Road.

- Knock him dead kid I'll be waiting and rooting for you.

Dabbed in his best attire from head to toe, a nice suit, shoes, and his satchel in hand enclosed with his Invisualator. It's there before a average building surrounded by no other property around a off road with the number of the address imprinted above the entrance in white sticker. The surface he observes is suspicious one corner after the other. His phone's GPS approves his place but doesn't resists him being twitchy about the location peeping around sure but unsure questioning to be there internally but any ill will feelings can be first time jitters in excuse. In he walks through the building seconds later in the most confident way the building seems to be completely deserted. Past a direction board beholding TIVOTU Nationalist. He ascends down some stairs where again there's no signs of life to a door where he turns the knob and enters. In he goes and first thing he sees is a modern room with four other people filling the seats. A breath escapes Merrill feeling more relaxed having seen the faces who return stares. He asks one is it there he approaches the desk for check-in where a woman sits no normal than a secretary at a doctor's office. The person, a female agrees. Merrill then turns to the woman for his meeting as schedule.

- Hello ! I received this letter in the mail that had invited me for...

- ...a interview.

- Yea..I get the feeling you were expecting me. My name is Merrill...

- Merrill Malenko, 4327 Casper, Alexandria Virginia. You have a 1:15...as you said we were expecting you.

- I can see...

He says. While scheming eyes behind her where there's a small pocket leading to a bridge of some doors where he catches a man larger than life in size exiting a room while stepping his way to the desk hawking Merrill the entire way. When he gets to the desk he plants down before the secretary a clipboard. She lifts and he sees taking his eyes off the intimidating figure and viewing the board brandishing a huge red letter "L". Odd and more than strange he thinks.

- Write your name down on the board and just have a seat until your called with the others.

He does and skims the list of names ahead of him on the board. That he minds before scribbling. Morrongiello, Mourning, Mowser, Mowry, and under goes his.

- Don't you mean separately, is this a group interview.

- Just have a seat Mr. Malenko. You all will be called shortly as to meeting your host for the evening. Thank you.

Flustered from all the questions and the secretary's weird dead on predictions he just abides and does as instructed. One of the visitors console his feelings that are more than mutual. As he sits before turning the dude big as a club bouncer apparently has never took one eye off him drifting away to his seat.

- Don't worry she did the same with me and even knew my social for some reason. Hey I'm Toussaint Mowry. Owner of the "Dynamo".

He introduces.

- Merrill Malenko, "Invisualator". I guess I'm not the only on a interview huh.

- Afraid not my friend, just about everybody here gunning for that fifteen mill. You get your letter in the mail.

- Yea right here, yours ?

- In my jacket pocket, I've been waiting for over a year for this meeting, I had two friends all went through this same process, and all had gone to bigger and better things. I suspect.

- Really, have I heard of them.

- Even I haven't yet it's only a matter of time since their houses sold. So that's a good sign. Anyways we're all pretend Thomas Jefferson's of our time. And I see your satchel so what does your toy do.

He asks.

- Oh it sees air...

- Air huh !

- ...and just about any bacteria drug infested in it.

- Wow, mines is a water generator. Can produce aqua within twenty minutes. I got these suckers check and mate in my pocket.

- Really...I guess only time will tell, wont it.

Says one of the other visitors side by them caressing her creation at her side.

A phone rings for the secretary, she answers normally. When finished she exits out into lobby to inform the visitors.

- Good evening to all guest. My name is Margaret. I will be escorting you all to your destination where your host awaits you. Here at TIVOTU we do things a little different when interviewing but fail no worry it isn't any harm than the usual. Although we do engage in groupings and it's only method to process our hiring stages much faster if you can bare. Today you will all be grouped by as "M". So please get a hold of your devices and follow me this way.

Rounded up they follow suit each visitor in a single file line through a dim hall to a door that sits last at the end. Before trolling in with her hand on the knob Margaret passes on another batch of instructions for them to take in high regard before entering in respects to the company's policy.

- Ok here we are group "M" this is the room. Now before stepping inside I want you to please keep your voices down, take a seat in the single row, and deliver all devices in front you before your legs. And one last thing, here beside this door there is this container during the process the host would like your undivided attention as to following. Which means no cell phones, ipods,or any communicative devices during this meeting.

Again feeling odd to this new experience, many even skeptical consider the company policy's during process and relinquish possession to their phones as permitted.

- We will get our phones back after right.

One of the guests assumes aloud. Margaret ignores the statement regardless how clear it was. She then opens the door to the room and one by one they fall inside their seat in this cold dark room where the only light glow hovers over the single seated row.

While everyone makes it to the seats with each creation at their shoe front's like explained. Finished to her objective, Margaret bids them a irregular farewell that caters to good luck. As they all are seated she pushes a button on the wall when exiting and calls to them all with their backs facing front with these last words before departure.

- Best wishes, Jespère que je vous reverrai.

She comments closing the door behind her.

Leaving the anticipation between the visitors in nerve wrecking suspense that can only be depleted through open expression from each guest.

- What the hell is this ?

- It's the interview idiot ?

- I've never had a interview like this ?

- Maybe it's a new practice ?

- I got a bad feeling ?

- Well maybe you should leave, give the rest of us a shot at that money. Huh ?
They all agree in unison.

- THERE IS NONE !

A unidentified boisterous voice says that brings to a end they're bickering and puts them all on alert in direction to the dark void before them.

- Who said that ?

Merrill asks calling into the darkness before them all.

- I did...

Out from the shadows in a sinister fashion, a man, dark in tone wearing a suit to ensemble his shade. Appears before them as his shoes clap against the floor in minor echo.

- Who are you ?

Toussaint asks.

- He's the host.

- Your reading is superb...I'm Rashid and before anything I want you all to know that it's most unpleasant to meet you fortunately in this stage.

- Was it you that said there is no money upon signing during this process.

- Yes I was.

- Wait no money, then what the hell are we here for then. Fuck this I'm outta here.

- Ah, Ah mister Mitchell...

Rashid says.

In the same instance out springs a man larger than life who grabs hold to the man like a doll in a bear hug grapple raising him off his feet and then easily carrying him back to his seat and placing him back in it like he would a child. Merrill and everyone stare in utter shock and disbelief at what has just happened before them. Leaving Rashid to only a few laughs while the man ventures to hawking Mitchell in a cold eye assuring things could be more dangerous for him if he tries that stunt once more.

- ...that's not how things go. And where are my manners excuse me, I like for you all to meet Abdullah and then his twin brother Abar. Both will be parlaying with us this evening making sure nothing unexpected is to happen during this process. Much like just a minute ago. I also feel fair in warning I must advise you align with your own appearance of the two gladiators that both men have capabilities well among your imagination may lead. I can only employ that any of you don't have the pleasure to experience any during our time here.

One snap to his finger in echo Rashid does signals to mechanizing the doors and enable their locks to latch in place by his call swiftly.

- Now with that out the way let me fill you all on how this works and why your here. Now first off like I said there is no money and never was, the letter sent to the each of you was a simple ploy for your appearance only and nothing more. And as tempted as we all can see you are it accomplished it's mission with supreme success...you all five are daily selects to taking advantage or using unneeded expenses to the world as we know it.

- What ?

Merrill cries.

- YOU ALL ARE IN DIRECT VIOLATION TO UNIVERSAL LAW AND CODE WITH MANIFESTING THESE DEVICES INTO THE WORLD AND MORE REPULSIVE WHOLESALING TO THE HIGHEST BIDDER.

- So what is this disciplining. You muthafuckas create a fake company to hold people accountable to your opinions of misdeeds.

- Not ours Ms. Mourning. As I stated this is universal law and code. Each of your meddling you've created with those machines you hold in front of you are to things you have no business tampering with. TIVOTU Nationalist. TIVOTU as in "Those in violation of the universe".

- Wait !...what are you going to do with us.

- Right I have a little boy at home.

- I have a daughter, please I can pay you anything you want. Just please let me go.

- Don't worry Mowry. Or any of you, TIVOTU Nationalist finds no pleasure in torturing those capitalistic and unworthy to fit into the correct order of things. In fact it's even willing to give you a second chance to make up for your unethical ways. So sort a speak you all will eventually get back to your family and children safe and sound, but it will depend entirely on you.

- What do you mean entirely on us. What are you going to do ?

Merrill asks.

- "What I'm going to do" is host. "What your going to do" is the essential question. And that question is nothing more simple than a test, quiz, or to the likes referred as a exam if you will.

- What kind of exam ?

Morrongiello asks.

- A moral challenge that will duel you all when the time presents itself whether physical, oral, multiple, reading, and even in written form during the moment to showcase how dutiful in person and character you truly are oppose to this shenanigan you've currently been flagged on. Those who will succeed, will, while those not... (laughs). Let's just get into it shall we people, first up we'll begin in contra order. That means you got first pickings Mr. Morrongiello, congratulations.

Released by the snap of Rashid's fingers goes the snaps from his chair as everyone looks on from his direction while both concierge figures put him on his feet latched on to both of his arms on both of his sides.

- Wonderful ! Ladies and gentlemen he'll be starting at our oral headquarters.

At the break of snapping his fingers one more time towards the pitch black fold behind him. Incomes a light above a room that resembles a classroom. Where he's escorted by the colossal men against his will. Merrill spots a bulge on both men's rear waist.

Inside the room he's place at a desk and locked in where a teacher figure steps inside and places a booklet and pencil before him. Looking on goes the others as a clock on the board holds five minutes, the teacher instructs him that he has five minutes to finish his course and when done, pencil's down. She instructs him to answer each question carefully reading and select the best answer afterwards. The clock begun after the instructions and Morrongiello answers all four questions within the booklet before the time is out. When finished the teacher then collects the book and proceeds to grading it out aloud for all to hear the announcing in fashion serving as the eve to his judgement.

- Now that mister Morrongiello has now completed his exam, it's time for the most exciting part during this process which is grading. Let's see what his grade is.

Rashid calls.

- Four questions. First. A homeless person asking for money for food. Do you think he deserves it ? He answered...Yes

Second question. If you saw a homeless person and they asked you for money to eat. Do they deserve your money ? He answered...no

Third. If you went to a school that prepared you for the world in every way. Do you think all people are entitled to that education ? He answered…yes.

Fourth. If you went to a school that prepared you for the world in every way. Do you think all people are entitled to that education even if you resent them ? He answered…no

The teacher voices out loud.

In only a matter of seconds she rounds up the grade and does announcing for them all to hear in suspense

- Each question answered correctly on the grading scale represents twenty five points. Mister Morrongiello was informed to answer four questions, he scored…zero. He failed.

The teacher voices.

Morrongiello confused and afterwards his temper flares at the teacher enraged confined to a children's desk as she exits the classroom. Not understanding the test in the first place while wondering what will happen to him next. Entering inside goes Abdullah and Abar at ease before him familiar to drill sergeants.

- Ladies and gentlemen mister Morrongiello was given four questions. If you observed the first question you'd realize that the second was in fact the same that equaled actually into only two questions, two questions that were the same and two questions he failed to pass. And here in TIVOTU Nationalist when you fail...

Sights are pointed at Morrongiello there in the class, out both men draw guns and let loose on him countless times shedding pieces of his flesh from the bullet tear before he dies tipped over within the desk still. Merrill and the others look in appalling fright as he's executed pitifully.

- ...you pay the piper, or in his case the bullet (laughs). Next in line goes Ms. Mourning come on down. For all of you who don't know Ms. Mourning is here for being responsible in creating a machine that actually allows her to hold time still but only for twenty minutes. And what does she do with this device she raids expensive clothing and jewelry stores to show off to friends so they can be jealous and envy of her upon sight. There's even rumors that she has more than one machine that performs the same.

Rashid snaps his finger no different than before while the two brothers remove her from her seat with tears streaming down her eyes as she begins to shout in resist although it does no good in her favor. She's escorted to the next room for the next quiz.

- Thank you Abdullah and Abar, she's fit and ready to take on the next exam.

- Your gonna kill her to.

Merrill asks out of spite.

- To kill doesn't option a choice, mister Malenko.

- This is fucking murder and you know it you sick fuck.

- No murder is unexpected, no matter of target, a gun to the victims head after the trigger is pulled and then they drop. Moving on to our next theme will cater to something Ms. Mourning is most familiar of.

Confined to a room pitch black with only two seats before a pole that has two red buttons on separate sides in the middle. Incomes the instructor who goes through the procedure with her as to the instructions of the exam.

Open is the room door incomes the host himself Rashid who goes and occupies the seat and red button on opposite sides of her. There as if he belongs, he listens on as herself to the following rules suppose.

- During this course you will be asked an amount of only four questions while both of you will be identified as seat A and seat B. Upon hearing there will be multiple answers for you to choose from that best will suit the question when asked, your duty is select the red button to answer before the other seat does. Listen carefully and pick the answer most compatible once heard. Does everyone understand ?

- Yes !

Rashid agrees.

- What questions ?

She asks unknowingly. But the instructor pays what she says no mind and then continues.

- Please let us begin.

The instructor says having dismissed her question. A game horn is aired to commence the exam.

- First question. In a capitalistic society what would be your goals in mind to achieving things more principle and harmonic overall ?
A. Succeeding
B. Reversing
C. Adapting
D. Surviving

Quickly after hearing not taking a ease Rashid slaps his hand on the red button to answer.

- Yes, seat A.

- B. Reversing

- Thank you, and all answers will be revealed afterwards.

Mourning envious to him being much faster stares on and is immediately drawn in the exam out of competitive nature. The second question goes underway.

- Second question. As a president in order to prevent a war, what is a most definite character trait needed for that person to possess.

A. Bargain
B. Negotiable
C. Reason
D. Strength

Once the question is spoken. Hands are tensed, first to slap their red button goes in surprise is Mourning. Eager to be first and arrogant as she shows rubbing it in Rashid's face in her own gloating demeanor.

- Seat B !

- The answer is D, strength. HA !

She answers in confident cockiness. The third question goes underway.

- Third question. If I allow one group to flourish but the other to wither, what word would I be.

A. Oppress
B. Deprive
C. Balancing
D. Wicked

Strike their button first goes again in repeated arrogance goes Ms. Mourning.

- C. Balancing

Looking on strapped down with nothing other to do but look on from their seats goes the others. Conversing amongst another is Merrill and Mowry.

- She gets this last one, I think she'll pass. What you think ?

Mowry says.

- No one is passing here.

He replies fierce.

- Fourth and final question everyone. What is the primary quality to freedom ?

A. Having
B. Taking
C. Asking
D. Wanting

Final answer and last stance in red button duel. Mourning comes in the finish.

- B, taking, like I just did.

Mourning in joy having finished her exam in confidence that she very well passed. Awaits the instructor to round up the answer in which were correct summing her outcome. He repeats each question and if right goes a bell in ring, wrong goes a alarm.

The first question goes in ring having Rashid answered. The second which Mourning answered goes in...a alarm. The third question which Mourning to answered goes in...a alarm. Final question she also scored as her hope has drained and uprise to fury goes...a alarm.

- Seat B you have officially failed your exam.

She screams in disappointment immediately and cries weeping the words "No, no, no" over and over. Looking each way for Abdullah and Abar expecting her fatality up next. Finally she finds herself alone with a spotlight hovering over her at the seat upon weeping. From behind she's snatched and dragged away by Abdullah. Kicking and screaming until finally he clinches his hand around her skull standing over her and twists her entire neck around "Voorhees style" tearing her head completely off. Nothing else to do the others just look on repulsive stunned in fear to their wildest dreams after seeing a man decapitate a women with his bare hands like he would a piece of fruit or a child would a toy. Commentating having a spotlight of his own goes Rashid.

- "As a president in order to prevent a war, what is a most definite character trait needed for that person to possess." Was the second question, and she answered what instructor ?

- I believe it was D, strength she chose.

- Well as we all just saw, and pardon my language ladies and gentlemen. Can't shit get stronger than that. Moving right along now...who's next. (Humorously)

He says returning to his original position before the remaining three strapped and confined to their seat most uncomfortably sane.

- ...ah we have the re-animator. Mister Mowser. Mister Mowser's responsibility being here is almost known more than any of you here. How ? because Mister Mowser has broke the code in re-generating, revitalizing, and most certainly resurrecting being. That's right... this man here is living proof to the "Herbert West" character. He created a synthetic tonic that if injected into one's pineal gland at the point of death it can bring a person back into the existence we know as life. He even was offered a million dollars by a lady that was in fact his neighbor who was dying of a rare heart disease to cure her. But he refused to treat her, didn't you Mowser.

- Why didn't you ?

Mowry asks Mowser venturing his eyes behind him to the door.

- That's a magnificent question mister Mowry to ask. Why did you turn away from helping that woman Mister Mowser when you knew she had lacking time from dying.

- Because I fucking hated her and that fucking dog she had that she wouldn't shut up, that wouldn't stop barking, or if wasn't barking it was infiltrating into my basement, my lab, and my work studies. And when I confronted her about it, she waved me off and it continued. So I'm supposed to help that. I don't think so, I didn't, I wont, and don't regret what I did either. You, her, them, them two darkies over there, or your fucking universe either.

Merrill and Mowry looks on at Mowser unimagined from his words that spring out of anger. Then towards Rashid who after hearing grins a big smirk over his face as he signals his straps to be unsecured. When they are right of away Mowser springs out of his seat and lunges in race to the door as he does all he can as to exiting as they look on in split disbelief and hope. Rashid does nothing but stand in his place looking on as he turns to any and every thought he can think as to prying himself out the door that's mechanically lock. Struggling in each attempt when he finally sees in pity, luckily advantage comes through and the door by some way comes ajar. Mowser's eyes excite when Rashid turns behind him and Abdullah sees handling a assault rifle in his hand that he aims through a scope targeting him there at the door. Recoil sprang in overwhelm power and before he can take a step passed the door squeezing through. A hole goes through him and knocks him to the floor. Impressive record shooting should be complimented.

It happens so fast that Rashid never even pays it any attention other than steady moving on to the last two standing guest.

- Mowser who ? Now only two. (Humorously)

The straps on Mowry commenced to loosen setting him free and exchanging him into the arms of both Abdullah and Abar who almost goes to dragging him from his seat as Merrill can do nothing but stare knowing that he too is next. Mowry while lifted off his feet can't do nothing but scream and holler in repeated words as he carried away hysterical "Wait a minute, just wait a minute." Rashid looking on can't help but to answer his cries.

- Oh for what Mowry, you've spent two years trying to get that water generator idea you had into the right hands for your payout. Now you don't want it anymore, your freedom back into society is worth more is that it...fine ok, I'll give it to you but you have to prove to them, how much you really want it back first.

- Prove to who ???

Mowry says being escorted into a room where the glass as it opens before him prints the letters across reading as " Parole board room". He's stuffed in a pitch black room in front of six people behind a desk while he's at his lonesome in a chair in front of them sensing his freedom is left upon their mercy in they're decision. The six representatives waste no time as well as empathy to his plea.

They prefer to ask him one question in importance that depends on the entire hearing and possibly his freedom.

- Mister Mowry we're going to make this as simple as possible there's no need to simmer through constant questions as to understanding or you displaying to us that you have now been fully rehabilitated and now are more equipped mentally, physically, and most importantly morally disciplined to be amongst the mass population once again. There's only one essential question that should be answered by you before the outcome ruled. And that is. Giving the opportunity, what would you do different before gaining your invitation here at TIVOTU Nationalist ?

Teary eyed and having heard the question that they've asked him the only answer in his head recaptures all that he's seen to the other guests once called to take their exams that none of them were left breathing or standing afterwards. He does all he can while weeping and moaning as to convincing them in his words that's he's entirely reconstructed and for a moral cause.

- There's so many things I literally would change having now went through this exam, sitting before all of you, and in this entire experience as a whole. I know for sure I would have urn for this so much as if my life depended on it, I wouldn't have never even created that stupid fucking water generator, and I wouldn't dare have disrespected the universe the way I now realized I have. I apologize for that and I only ask, no I beg of you all for just one second chance to correct my wrong and reverse my faults.

The representatives observe him all at once, looking at him but more through him trying to take in whether or not he truly is remorseful in his role that has brought him here. Majority look convinced and they begin to steer to end the meeting.

- I as well as my other board members here are gracious Mister Mowry as to here you pour out your heart in honesty in dear sincerity. And I'm going to grant you a approval to be set free, I'm most definitely confident you've learned a valuable lesson from this encounter here today. And I believe my colleagues are aligned no different.

- I concur. In fact I'll go as far as to granting you something even more special that intertwine to the moment.

- Thank you all, and sir whatever it is I would be most grateful.

- How would you feel if I granted you the indeed fifteen million dollars here for your device upon your exit.

- I'd feel I don't know, if you insist ?

He says. Before his dismissal the representative scribbles down on a small note and waves it in his direction saying.

- Ok mister Mowry your parole has been granted. Here's your check, follow the exit sign out.

Merrill from his seat looks on almost in disbelief almost as if he can't believe what he sees. Mowry steps to the desk and places his hand on the check along with the representative issuing. But when he doesn't let it go. He gives him a look before the board as he tells Mowry one last thing when he finally does.

- Congratulations son, but I never said you passed your exam.

Confusion spreads over his face like diseased. Over the desk on both of his sides incomes both Abdullah and Abar blitzing his body over good with bats until he hits the floor. The board members depart the room all at once as he's beaten into a pulp then his death.

Rashid bids farewell to a pummeled Mowry one last time as he's no longer breathing and dragged away breathless into the darkness. Leaving Merrill as the lone survivor and undeniably helpless to his fate awaiting him at his approach to his upcoming exam just as the others.

- It's been a long and unsuccessful day. Four guest and four disappointments. I always thought wisdom came with redemption. But it looks like my philosophies to my are only sayings and nothing more. However, maybe coming in last you can turn that around for me Malenko. You can certify my statement to being accurate unlike the others.

- Or you can just stalk, wait for your opportune, and strike.

- Is that what I been doing ?

- This entire fucking project. You didn't bring any of us here for redemption or second chance for what we've done. You came to do what you did since we stepped in this got damn room. And I'm no different... so let's get this shit over with.

- Well that's something you got going for yourself Malenko. And I haven't seen this all day, it's called "honorable confrontation" this was unexpected. But let's see where it gets you.

His straps unreleased him and on arrival in like timing comes both Abdullah and Abar from each side snagging him away in that infamous stroll as he watched the others be lugged in path to their exam quarters. Question is will he prevail ? Or will he become a mother victim collected as all the others.

Pushed within a room by the two muscles and then to have the door locked behind him. Merrill panics on fright to where he's stored in darkness. Banging on the door, calling and pleading for it to be opened, in a consistent of repeats. Until a spotlight shines on his back for attention and turns around to view the atmosphere to which he's confined. He steps closer to the light and then finally he finds himself walking before a podium where he looks out before and he sees a audience of people that consist into the thousands. Ascending down the aisle with a microphone goes Rashid who announces his exam instructions in specific sincerity as the large audience stare on in complete silence. Like they've came to see him perform and won't leave until their satisfaction is giving.

- Right here and now on the spot, you tell how this experience has changed you. Since you have so much confidence, I figure what good of a judge than a few people oppose to an audience. If you can convince them honestly, no games, no tricks, or deceit this time you've passed. So let's go we're all waiting on you Mister Malenko.

Looking out into that audience is enough to enhance stage fright into stage death.

Merrill keeps cool and does the only thing having feeling the intuition at moment.

- Uh....uh...I'm not good at the center of attention but I guess I'll have to make a exception being that my life depends entirely on this. I've witnessed four people who I didn't even know literally murdered in front of me. First thing that comes to my mind seeing that shocks you into horror and you empathize with the victims saying to yourself that they didn't deserve it. But now realizing I see what each of their exams represented and enticed to bring out of them when we didn't. Although the guests didn't possess that one trait. I'm talking about ethics, our main objective hear was because we were violators of the natural way of things and now we're getting our comeuppance for it. You don't use vital secrets of the world in exploitation for your own benefits and expect to get away with it. We all were at wrong including myself. I was told to convince you all into giving me my judgement but I'm not going to do that. Now I believe each everyone of you should come to whatever conclusion you pose best suitable for my sins and I'm ready to take sole responsibility for them without a doubt. Most important thing I learned here today, here in this experience is and always will be is MORALITY. Respect for one self, the creator, and the universe especially.

When he finishes a round of applause tunes the audience into they all fade and only person left clapping is none other than Rashid. The room as he stood faced to a podium that Merrill once knew has now taken a transition that lends him face to face in a dark room before the host in conclusion to his appeasing speech. Rashid expresses his feelings toward his exam presentation.

- It took a full cast but at least one came out with the exact emphasis of this whole experiment. It's good to see Mister Malenko. People have to realize that the world isn't their oyster, it isn't here to manipulate, mistreat, or control for their own material wants. That isn't what we're here for. During our inception a purpose is spawned on to us to complete for a greater good of ourselves and most important the society we come amongst. Any violations in our behavior will perpetuate the same results on to others which will catapult a world esteemed into negativity. Where evil and wickedness rang in abundance, so much so it becomes an epidemic, a way of life, a way of wrong, a way of immorality.

- I understand.

- I can see now...and I hope this is the first and last time myself and the TIVOTU Nationalist establishment is to ever lay eyes on your name and face again. And hint to confidentiality of universal order as to regulating and installing proper structure to the world.

- Oh trust me if there's anything I will most definitely keep, it's this experience, and those words embedded into my personality every step of the way for now on.

Unlock goes the door from where he came out that springs the beauty of daylight pried open by the two brothers of destruction. It's time for Merrill as the last and only survivor to finally having finished to go home. Past him Rashid the host allows him his path in way through the doors after shaking his hand firmly in farewell. In good spirits before the light hits looking back Rashid asks. That turns Merrill back around to hear.

- Its a whole new world. I'm curious what is the first thing your going to do when you get back out there.

- After destroying that device, I'll write a book on everything that I experienced here today.

A smirk in devious behind his ordinary expression occurs to Merrill. A minute shared between the two happens as a smile inflicts both before a suspected goodbye is likely. But never shows, hearing Merrill's response wasn't a ploy for harmless curiosity but more to solidified his reconstruction was complete. When its clear, it isn't. Fast Rashid goes into removing a gun from behind his waist and explodes endless rounds in direction toward him cutting him down in execution, not even leaving his blood to be exposed to the sunshine. As both Abdullah and Abar pry back shut the door and cling to dragging his body away. While Rashid leaves one last word in epilogue, detaching the empty magazine while the barrel blows smoking hot.

- VIOLATORS !

THE END

DEPRI-enteritis

TEXAS

Near in middle age goes a man well suited in a tie and jacket that coincides to his sharp dark hue takes a seat inside a room space within a ordinary bank gleaming joy in his eyes and determination in his presence. Armed with a portfolio as he sits across a youthful broker doing the handling. The representative to the local headquarters with his name blazing off his pin tag from his jacket is "Wiley". And he wastes no time into getting to the point regarding their appointment and the current status between just the two of them and what looks to involve a case with obtaining a loan.

Before the exchange of words the older man slides over having nearly forgotten the portfolio to the man servicing him behind the desk.

- Excuse me, I'm so nervous I forgot to give you the papers the other day you asked for. Inside are both three months of my pay stubs, social security, license, and apartment rental credit. They're xeroxed and copied too.

He gets out of the way.

The broker stares down at the portfolio without touching after it placed in front of him and immediately his face paints dread and unfortunate.

- First Mr. Henry, now you and me have talked and we have discussed between the two of us that this attempt in obtaining your loan from here might be a little too exuberant for us to allow to someone such as yourself...

- Yea I knew that coming in but I discussed with Mr. Johannsson before I was transferred to you that he had informed me that so long as I had all the proper paperwork and could provide proof in any area needed. I should be fine, correct ?

- I understand and realize how patient you've been with us and there's nothing more than myself personally would like to see other than yourself obtaining the plumbing company that you filed for. But unfortunately at this time we just cannot option out that specific amount to you giving to the reason that you've never really taken on this particular role as sole ownership before. This is big risk for us.

- So your denying me the loan.

- Believe me, I know how you feel at this moment but trust and believe maybe you should tried your chances in a year or so, maybe when you've gained enough experience as a owner or perhaps file with a different bank.

- How the fuck am I suppose gain experience at being a owner when you wont even allow me the loan that I filed for initially here at this one. I was suppose to be meeting with the space owner for my headquarters in a hour, then a broker for a job over in Beaumont afterwards. And now your hear telling me I'm being denied for the loan, right. What's the real reason ?

- There are none Mr. Henry these things happen sir, but I'm willing to bet you if you try another time that maybe things will bargain to your favor.

- ARE YOU DENYING ME FOR THE LOAN, YES OR NO.

- Yes, unfortunately yes...

The gentleman drops his head in distress, form his hands to one as they lock into each other. He then shifts his head away from the desk while Wiley further consoles him after denial.

- ...some words of advice if I were you I'd try another bank I'm sure they'll be...

- ...they'll be more than willing as to escorting you through a new case that'll possibly be rewarding for you.

He finishes his sentence as if the phrase has been reiterated to him before again and again. While Wiley sorts through the paperwork and finds several other applications from other banks. Instincts drive him toward Mr. Henry who he shifts from the prior position and back geared toward him and the look in his eye charges in great animosity but before Wiley can prepare. Jolts in leaps from his seat incredibly goes Mr. Henry across his desk and he attacks him beastly in the midst to his speech.

LOS ANGELES

Residing within a building space that's newly being processed during its construction goes a worker in disagreement with his superior side by him who isn't wise enough to take in consideration his idea of which way to run the water pipe that's according to the blueprints. The supervisor advises him to slightly change the plans on account of how he prefers it oppose to how it's suppose. Back and forth the argument carries until his supervisor insists for someone else to do the job as he calls a new worker to the task but as he turns his back the worker balling his bronze fist angrily snatches in his reach a pipe and he swings it before his superior can make a call out in the hall for someone new. The pipe swipes a blow to his head and knocks him over by a electric machine used to cut steel and cast iron parts. Not unconscious, his boss struggling to make to his feet from the fall. The worker yanks his arm and rests it under the machine and flicks it on as the blade runs fast as he cries for help knowing what's underway. It transitions in unheard male screams when he lowers the spinning blade on his arm and it buries speedily grotesque into his flesh, running blood all over. Entering the works of the beginning stages to sever him alive.

NEW YORK

Within a office building a concierge prioritizing to her daily duties seems a bit agitated while engaged with several guests scheduled for visits in the building's suite floors. But giving the reason before gaining access to the spaces they must provide identification that solidifies their presence is valid. But when doing so many of the tenants and guests feel the need in strange habit as to when releasing her they're I.D. cards rather than physically handing them over. The game that they play is suspecting when they insist to sliding it over instead. The young concierge recognizes it as a form of disrespect and out of spite she does the same in return when finishing skimming over the photos and names one after the other. During this process a regular tenant eyeing when coming off the elevator sees her move and locks eyes with the concierge as the two both share friction in each gaze. When turning the corner in route to their floor it just so happens the tenant bumps into the girl's supervisor and informs by whisper all that he had seen. She assures that it'll be taken care of without any worries as he approves.

Later in the day around lunch the concierge suffers the same issue with now a new guest only but this time there's a little more eyes on her and in particular it lands on being her supervisor having arriving on the scene returning from break, she sees what happens but pays it no mind. Stepping off the elevator the very same tenant who pointed out the conduct, locks eyes with the supervisor firm to assure whether or not the situation is rightfully taken care of. In reminder off glance, the supervisor after the guest is allowed access the concierge takes her seat down while sighing out of distress and annoyance having along with happening to notice a noisy tenant looking over briefly. She hears it from her superior as she tells.

- Singer, please next time when your finished with obtaining the guests cards place them back into their hands and do not slide them over. It looks unprofessional and I've received a complaint from a tenant who noticed.

The concierge set tight in her ways of developing more than agitation that is clearly well within her demeanor. Her head twists another direction which makes her appear to ignore the comment made, her back is slump down, her hand becomes connected with the other as she interlocks them for a second. Not hard for her supervisor to see this escalating, quickly she just decides on asking whether or not she got the point she was alluding to.

- Be careful next time because any other complaints can lead to a write up. You understand ?

The young girl in her sight catches a pen that's on the table she uses to sign in her guest. Ripping it away from the table in acceleration she stands to her feet after being called by her name repeatedly. Her stance fears her supervisor to step back from the confrontation having brushed over the look in her eye. The concierge goes in for the attack there in the lobby and begins to impale the pen over and over on her body as the supervisor screams leaving tenants appalled and nothing to do but run for help or look in cringe as blood shoots all over before she hits the floor.

It's there the girl infused with her rage steers in direction to the very tenant who informed the supervisor standing there. Wasting no time she rushes over in demented steps performing pursuance to a killer into his direction as fright claims his knees to run but only screams pour from him she waves the bloody pen prior used now at him as people scatter in tremble knowing he's next.

WASHINGTON D.C.

Locked off within a office a chief goes over these weird cases of murderous freak occurrence's popping up all over with his best investigator in assured hopes that he'll solve this horror raged jinx before it explodes even more out of their entities handling.

- New rebel rousers have showed up and best believe these bastards are calling for ordinary joes blood. Killed some people and didn't stop to their was nothing left but their mutilated, unforeseen bodies. It happen in a course of three regions all now documented at the very same time. West, south, and east. Total chaos, I just gotta a call on the goddamn horn that there's more of the same exact cases showing up everywhere like a fucking epidemic. I want to know what's going on, it's my job to know what's going on. What is this, who the fuck in this god loving country has the balls or spirit to bring this misery to our house in the good ol' U.S of A.

- What is it a virus, illness, a contagion ?

- We don't know and to be honest with you I really don't give two shits son, my job is to find out and neutralize the fucking problem before more innocent people have to lay out in the street dead like a fucking dog because of some beastly maniacs, who think the world is just going to get out of their. But they can forget it, the same rules apply to everyone, no savagery. That's why I have you hear Davis, I need something and I need you get out there and get it for me so we can blow whatever the fuck this is the fuck back where it came from. Can you do that for me son.

- If I couldn't Captain I wouldn't be here now would I sir.

- That's what the hell I like to hear. Suit up, we need you out in 0800 hours.

V.O

[Name, Deion Davis. Reside, District of Columbia. Career ? I spent eight years as a private investigator. The city's best. I spent almost a decade trying to find any and every person brought across me. Muggers, killers, psychos, wackos, rapist, crooked politicians, any and all. If their file hit my desk, my fee was paid, then you got what you were looking for. I'm reliable without fail there's even a rumor or two that I'm what they call a "skilled". I'll take any case but this one was different, ordinary people with ordinary jobs murdering co-workers uncontrollably ? Doesn't make sense and even worst their all linked in occurrence which means much more for me to carry and to figure out. I sought out the families and the files for the first attack in Texas before things intensified.]

Screams cry out in a cloud of madness as a crowd look on in fear as a man in a fit channeled obsessively by some kind of unforeseen rage. Strangle another with his belt before a gated community while the man near death scrape and claw his way in attempts to unleash the leather strap from his neck for oxygen. His eyes water and the veins by his whites transition from pink to red, spectators look on or dash away into their houses. Some take cover can't bear to watch as the man's life goes in countdown before he tires and withers off by the great grips of the madman grunting and squeezing as the belt grows tighter and tighter shutting off his victims circulation.

Police arrive on the scene before the man's departure when a few neighbors step in and tackle the enraged man down. It doesn't do any better as he now commences to pounding his fist over the men one by one as he's too much for their control that many just breakaway while one remains helpless to his psychotic fury. Straggling away coughing for new breaths is his original victim as the police arrive and views, observing the altercation in plain as a black man pummels a white man inching to his death. One of the cops demand for back up from his other officer as his warning shots and command don't yield away his aggressive behavior.

The other cop races to the squad car as he screams over the radio at what he saw. While the other at the scene ask a bystander in near what had taken place to cause his eruption.

- We don't know, I saw the guard refuse him to pass so I guess he snapped.

Watching the man swing his fists like sludge hammers over the man he mounts. Bystanders look on and excite the cop to shoot him but frantic he is at the man's acting. He points his gun in the air and still too weak to squeeze a round. Cowardly in his ways he just simply sprints away back to the car where he charges at his partner so frightened for the radio, he literally snatches it away from his hand disrespectfully. Insult spreads his face, a look in rage spills over him as he twists his neck the opposite direction as the cop eases his hand to his holster at his waist. Almost as he's swapped to a completely different person. Turning to him for confirmation of the problem in response to the radio dispatcher on the other side they aid to. When he does the insulted cop turns around with both hands in kill mode wrapped around his standard issue pointed directly at his forward. Before he can blink the trigger is pulled for all nearby to hear in more screams.

Davis seated down with the wife and sister of the man originally from the bank. The explain they don't know what would come over him to have him overreact in the way that he did to what the police had claimed.

- I don't believe any of it at all investigator. I mean I knew my husband for twenty-two years and I have never even seen him as to raise his hand to a mouse the way they depicted him. Not my Travis, he's a worker and dedicated. It was his dream to start his own plumbing business and now there's sayings he's responsible for murder. I mean I don't get it.

- Myself either, I mean we both seen him this morning before he ran off to the bank. He looked completely fine, no signs of a temper or rage set on him like the cop who had informed us claimed.

- So he was on his way to the bank for a loan. Anything else.

- He had a meeting with some other contractors I believe to obtain the first job for his company but I can't remember what time he told me.

- Ok...ok, thank you both. And please take my card make sure you contact me if Travis returns here, anytime of the day or night. Please call me, because the average police get a hold of him they won't be as gentle as I will.

He states.

When Davis finishes his question and answer routine he collects enough evidence and clues for him to perhaps connect pieces to explain things later pinned to a note pad. He departs the residence on some foundation but a call he gets from a trusty puts him a little more further to things.

One of his coroner buddies get there hands on one of the madmen cases. He buys him off with some cash and looks over the body for himself. He observes the lifeless vessel in all detailed regions as it resembles nothing out of the ordinary almost like nothings wrong other than the bullet wounds to his chest and neck. Davis after spotting does his best to reenacting, then realizes how strange it is to see a man that's slightly young, black, and said to have a possessed tantrum so volatile only though it never shows it.

Finally he makes a call to another friend for another favor in desperation to perform a special autopsy on the body. While he goes out of town to L.A. to question the wife of the construction worker. The west coast spark in this massacre trifecta.

- Tanner it's Davis.

- Heeey D wasup, what you need ?

- I'm cool, but I do need something ?

- Go ahead.

- I need a inspection on a body thoroughly. Brain, heart, blood, the works. Anything you can possibly find.

- Any specifics on what your looking for ?

- I can't pinpoint as of yet. But I'll let you make that guess after seeing it.

- Hey D, this wouldn't be one of those civilians turn savage pieces is it.

- How'd you know ?

- I just got two in a hour ago, and another coming right as we speak.

- Find any conclusions.

- Not yet, but when I do your on my list first for the update.

- Kool ! Thanks !

Ending that call incomes another from Maher in emergency upon hearing the tone of his voice. It's clear whatever problems previous must've have spiral more deeper. His captain urges him to get to a television, outside the coroner office he exits to the hospital lobby where he gets a glimpse to the waiting room set open to the awaiting patients. It's there he sees it flashed before the screen holding all eyes within the facility at a dramatic halt to attention in viewing the afternoon news.

Headlines read "Bedlam at the House, several casualties for seat holders upon meeting". According to the story that Maher explains as best as could displaced by his fear.

A confidential meeting had taken place with about six seat holders discussing plans on ordering a new act to punish offenders of the law that publicly conduct violence. The conference was disclosed to only a few that was selected and as it was said that solutions into eliminating the problem waved over in the meeting by many. Only with Jim Sly a southern state seat holder felt to be overlooked as his ideas constantly fell on death ears to which he thought or we're even more disrespectfully over talked once he brought them up. After showing his dislike for the rude gestures, the veteran participant expressed his feelings toward their negating. Instead of a apology a despicable joke in regards to his appearance and placing there being set solely on tokenism is revealed by the house's whip. Immediate laughter and giggles spread the room and as the veteran rep goes to respond he becomes froze, he tucks his head, sudden shakes come over him until he's stuck looking away from the group as their smiles dissolve realizing his odd gestures aren't that humorous as before. Finally they call his name and he stands funny and weird and he goes forth to one of the podiums inside and grips firm tight on the handle of a gavel. Turns around and strikes fast in step toward the house whip and repeatedly begins to drive the wooden hammer to his head as screams come over all in the room as many begin to scatter as the whip lay dead after a few pounds as the splatter make a mess over the veterans suit. A care not to his mind only claiming the others sight which is what he did until the secret service was called to put him down.

Maher urges for Davis to step on the pace on the trail to diagnosing the problem. Divesting the theory to be of a virus perhaps like once before. Davis does all the convincing he can next as to informing he's on the investigation before departing the call.

In route to his flight as he passes through security the officers awaiting announces directly to Davis to not aboard with his drink or food.

- Excuse me sir, please do not sneak through the detector with any food or beverage.

Security presumes.

Frustration boils over him as he goes to explaining.

- Relax I'm a investigator for the department.

He returns reaching for his badge to display in proof.

- I understand sir, but still regulation policies informed clearly that no food or beverages are permitted or allowed entering through security check. Regardless anyone who's boarding.

Security states.

Davis doesn't argue, and does like instructed and he empties his food and drink into a nearby trash as he's finally allowed through. Meanwhile a Caucasian couple with their son is awarded access with no fuss even as the son and wife maintain bottled drinks.

When passing the detector a man behind the couple is then harassed after they depart in pursuit to their flight for chewing gun. When ask to empty the piece he asks for a explanation from security as to why he's being harassed when not a word was mention to the family before him as they clearly possessed drinks. Davis looks on as they disregards his statement and he sense their next move will most certainly lead to detaining him for his commotion. Other looks on at his outcry from injustice stick in the air while a few guards approach the scene crowding him. Davis sees and interferes purposely, with a few flashes to his badge he convinces them to allow the man through under his supervision.

Arriving in Los Angeles he meets with the wife of the construction worker who recites the same and identical story as to having no expectance by her husbands actions no different than the case in Texas. Hinting to him being under stress by his job but nothing to push him overboard as to doing what he did, Davis makes note of. Arrangements to look over his body after being gunned down following his act Davis has with the coroner as he escorts him personally to the suspect and he goes through his observance peeping for any interesting detail on his body. The coroner insists on staying through his procedure, that leads to several vital clues that could later be potential strong points in cracking his case.

- Your an investigator, right !

- That's what my credentials say, eight years in.

 - How long on this case ?

- A couple days at the most. Just trying put pieces together, following every clue in detail.

- Really ? Tell me something ? What did you find so far...just at the sake of curiosity. Between a coroner and a detective.

- The average intel that seem to always intertwine in the beginning. When your a investigator it's no different than a puzzle. One big ass puzzle, a lot of people think it takes intelligence and wit in order to discover where each piece goes biggest to smallest in order to finish...

- If not, then what it is ?

- Well if it isn't smarts or brilliance to sum up the true outcome than in my estimate. Eight years in business, private contracting, every file that came across my desk that I indeed solved on my own. It was one word...PERSISTENCE. Take this case in example only three to four days on the file and already I figured out each suspect pretty much were average people who exploded in the same fit in the very same day in three major regions of the world without any motive to do so. So the only thing now is to find out what and how this occurrence came about so sudden. And where does it come from, is it contagious, a illness that occurs naturally, or possibly airborne. A even interesting clue come to think is each individual subjected were in fact black.

- What if it was mental ?

- What do you mean ?

- I mean these cases are popping up more and more with no answers, clues, or analysis. What if I told you the reasoning resided in each of individual's mental space during the moment.

- How do know ?

Davis asks.

- Let me show you something.

He follows the coroner over to another body he's already given an autopsy on from it's organs thoroughly. Tearing the white sheet from a body no different than the construction worker. The coroner with ease and no squirming removes the skull of the corpse to reveal the brain of the body. He squats as Davis mimics him the same and flashes a light over the brain wielding a knife instrument in his hand while explaining first.

- Are you familiar with the brain.

- No ?

- Don't worry at least your honest, but here it is. Our brain has two portions a left hemisphere and then naturally the right. In both sections they're responsible for our most greatest functions from physical to mental. The hypothalamus is what it's called, it stimulates all controlling behavior. From sexual arouse, urge to eat, drink, sleep, it even controls your body temperature. But more specifically it regulates your emotions, how do you feel or think about certain things. Now it's located here.

He says while reaching to the specific area within the organ and exposing it to Davis.

- What does this mean ? What are you implying ?

- I don't know as of yet but what I do know is if you pay attention to this area in this individual, then the other cases that are same. In comparison to a ordinary body the appearance and consistency is completely off. Look.

He calls to while revealing other cases like the construction worker or the man in Texas and their hypothalamus's looking borderline to deterioration almost as if there slowly decreasing. Loosing it's shade, size, and supposing feel indifferent to any other body that hasn't took on those symptoms and extreme confrontational behavior.

- I don't understand, it's almost like these areas in their brain are being detained, restrained...

- DEPRIVED.

The coroner adds.

Having left the coroner's office and adding that interesting piece of research and theory to his investigation as it sticks with him. In his hotel room looking over papers analyzing the three main cases and several others almost in exact. He near calls it a night as he rests before the television as a story waves across the screen that drives him to arising out of his comfort position about chaos erupting at a school where more than a dozen students inside one school attacked their teachers in more than ten classrooms near the same time. Leaving only one teacher as a survivor after and the school facility now being overpowered by the students. Davis connects the story to his case as he sits there to ponder on what will become of this new mysterious social plague beginning to spread in epidemic.

There in his office staring beyond the view of his city within the nation's capital. Stands Maher shedding a expression over his face that reveals utter disgust and contempt to the sound of a police scanner that blares throughout his office of numerous situation after situation that all relate to very symptoms to qualify as the mystery plague. Finally after hearing it continuously, a aid of his shuts it off with his intentions to further explain how serious a problem they have on their hands with this major public emergency.

- The calls have now sunk down from every thirty minutes to now every eight to ten. We can't stop this, not like this captain. Which can only mean by tomorrow...

- ...that whatever the fuck this is would have soared beyond our containment leaving us in a inferior position. While they reign in dominance.

- Only if...

He says as a pause settle between the two. Before the general turns facing his aid to word.

- You take care of it.

- Done !

The aid wastes not even a second as to responding to his orders to greenlight the situation. Then quickly exiting the office leaving the captain to his lonely of worried wondering as he turns before his office view, reaches in his pocket, pulls from his phone and to one number, one person, one individual intending to call, Davis.

Having departed from his flight, exit Davis goes through the airline walk area, into the outside airline terminal where he tries his luck to flagging down a cab but it'll take damn there a miracle in his case for that trick to occur as many intend to overlook his calls as he sprout his hand in the air to signal but inappropriately they only jet by in ignore.

Detecting the resistance perhaps collided with the prejudice famously known to New York cab's reputation. He moves along further down and happens to stumble before a cab parked at the curb. He looks to the front seat and sees the driver occupied and sneaks himself into the backseat. Surprise to him there's already a passenger there. A downtown attorney type draped in a suit and raincoat, who gives a eye to in discomfort once Davis presence enters. The man doesn't hold back his distaste to sharing a cab either voicing it under his breath.

- Great, another one I have to share a cab with. Let's get a move on would you, I have a important conference call in forty-five minutes. Manhattan square step on it.

The passenger turning red in the face says.

The driver's dark eyes flashes through the mirror displaying the youth in his eyes turning to the red face passenger and then to Davis who looks over and recites his destination following.

- St. Vincent's Hospital.

Davis says.

The driver muted from discussion is once again hassled by this disgruntled red face passenger who deeply encourages for him to depart. Finally the cabbie does but his verbal lashing doesn't cease there. On and off through the ride he holds nothing back as to chastising the driver for his decisions in navigation. He doesn't like this turn, or that turn, this street, or that street. Even going off at his mouth as to stating why the driver felt the need to head in the route that he followed. Looking on does Davis as every time the passenger goes to open his mouth he cringes in annoyance looking on at the cabbie in empathy having to have to put up with the person and probably take on this social punishment on the daily basis. But finally after taking as much as he could the younger driver clashes back at a light to the harassment.

- Look man if you have a problem on how I operate this vehicle, my vehicle, you don't have to stay in here because I had enough of your bickering at me, I'm not your child.

- I'm closing in on losing one of the most expensive deals within this city on account this fucking loser. THANK YOU very much.

Blatantly disregarding the driver's last comment as if he never made it occupied to his phone.

Davis shakes his head in disgust while the driver hand twitches out of his control against the wheel that comes unknowingly as he swerves in the street to his surprise. The calls become greater from the red face passenger after the move, the young driver begins to look distressed winding his neck like he wants to turn his head behind him strangely. Davis takes notice immediately and compliments the gestures to his frustration boiling. His instincts feeling to make a response in he dives into the harassing to disgust the belligerent passenger's tyrant behavior uncalled for in a simple taxi ride.

- Leave the fucking kid alone and let him drive. He a cabbie not your personal nigga horse and carriage.

- As long as I'm paying him and I'm in this vehicle I'm entitled to use any phrase or word I care to say from my mouth that's no concern of yours. Who the hell are you suppose to be anyway ?

The passenger responds boldly.

Reflex tunes Davis that isn't even exact to the point in expressing as he whips out his pistol and presses it cold at the red faced passenger's temple. No luck to him he never saw it coming as he reached into his pocket with his hand on a pack of cigarettes. Davis tosses his badge in his lap and demands that he recites the embedded text within the gold shield. As he insist himself unto his pockets having removing the cigarettes himself.

- Read it... or it'll be your brains painted in this back seat that'll fill in for you at your conference meeting not you.

- District of Columbia, private investigator.

He says without any restrain.

- That's who I am...

Snatching back his badge, the cabbie focus on the road and hears every bit of what happened in surprise.

- ...now you said as your paying him and your inside this vehicle your allowed to say whatever it is you wish without my concern.

- Correct, look just take it easy. I got a three month year old kid I'm trying to get home to, alright.

- Really, so do you talk to your kid like you just talked to that kid over there. Apologize.

He commands.

The red face passenger does as told frightened by Davis perhaps pulling the trigger, so he agrees without question and he apologizes to the young cabbie. Following the apology Davis request that the driver pull the car over, he makes the passenger pay his correct fare for the ride and a most pleasing tip for his harassing mouth the entire way. When he's finished, he kicks him out the car and makes him walk the rest of the way. After pulling off he tosses out his cigarettes leftover to be his company during the hike.

Disbelief to his outstanding assistance the cabbie feels indebted to Davis as he tries to consume what had just happen. What to do, how to feel, what to think. Humbly all that comes out is.

- Thank you !

- It's nothing young man.

As personal aid and instructed directly by Maher himself his loyal officer having informed the platoon of troops and now in the beginning stages to deploy the streets to return order back into the infrastructure's possession. He gives the men another five minutes to prepare before heading out on duty after his detailed objective is went over for everyone on board to follow properly. Urging at his pockets he notices he's misplaced his cell phone so his first thought is to check the vehicle in near leaving his post. It's there he finds it alongside his M4 automatic rifle. Right of way he sends a message to his wife that words over the screen "With patience opens chance ". On his way in returning he hears a voice that waves over to the men almost to instructing. Curious the aid sees another officer at his post so he surges back and interrupts the announcing momentarily as he pulls the officer to the side.

- What are you doing ?

- What I was instructed.

- I'm giving the orders within this operation. I'm on direct permission from captain Maher himself, and I'm going make sure directly after this he hears about this so you can personally be drawn up on charges in grounds to insubordination.

- Is that so, because it just so happens he informed me with this message last minute and permitted me to inform you as well as anyone else if needed to.

The officer replies revealing his device that prints loud and clear from their very superior in these words "Take the lead, any refusal pass on this message."

Disappointment overwhelms the aid as he steps aside normally and respectfully while the other officer returns to post and continues announcing his objective that's sided with a sinister grin. The aid routes himself away in a shattered trance after being disregarded. Having returning to his vehicle briefly and then once more back to post fidgeting away to a object in his hand. Positioning himself behind the implanted officer seems to be almost intentional when eyes of the soldiers become aware to his doings, it's too late. There he finds himself behind the last minute implanted officer and a spray of bullets shower him and the entire room along with it from his M4 he retrieved.

Davis inside the coroner's room is fortunate just as in Los Angeles where he's showed the exact area along the brain's hypothalamus where it displays great deficiency by the coroner. When finished he receives a call coincidentally finally from his friend who's the coroner back home in update to the results of the now epidemic. Davis previously enlightened beats to him the results detailing.

- Yea !

- Good news, I found your conclusion on what's causing this behavior in all these cases.

- Hypo-thalamus, I know.

- What the hell ? You performing autopsy on the side when you not investigating.

- You can say in regards to this case on.

- Yea but that's not the only thing. It's getting out of control and becoming more and more a problem especially here. I got so many bodies here from cops than the maniacs. Its getting to the point where I'm beginning to have to look for help out of town. But I did some research and need you and only you here to reveal it. How soon can you get here.

- I'm in New York now, I'll take the first flight out.

- I'll be waiting.

Tearing in huge knocks like they can come through the door. Answer goes Maher as he sees a few of his soldiers disoriented in fright. Panting and barely can hold breath as they barge into his office and locks the door behind him in tension hysteria as one goes to explain what occurred. It's then Maher visions them and their uniform covered in blood naturally his first response is.

- What happened ? What going on ? That's a order right now.

- Sir he did it, I don't know if there's anymore survivors other than us. We're lucky to even be fucking alive.

- Who did what ?

- Mercer sir, he went ballistic. See he had some words with Schlepps and then came back and just started shooting. We all watched him tear into Schlepps and everyone else. HE'S GOT IT !!!

- Is he dead ?

- We all just ran after that.

- Is he dead ?

- I never seen anything like that in my fucking life sir, his face seem like it just had no emotion or empathy when he fired.

- IS HE DEAD ?

- We don't know...sir.

A different soldier intervening claims.

- Somebody get Davis ass on the phone right now, tell him get his ass down here. It's time to put a end to this shit once and for all right now.

Cruising the block in a uber Davis after landing from his flight, pictures first hand what this condition that has now infected thousands or maybe millions of others has now did within his city. There's patrol cruisers occupying half city blocks all over every turn in the downtown area. Many caution tapes scenes are too viewed by him. Seeing what can be perceived as blood spilled all over one sidewalk passing through a light. Then a couple paces down from his destination two paramedics are seen exiting a building blocks away from the white house strolling a stretcher with the object covered in white sheets Davis stares closely in transit. There's a second team of paramedic following behind with yet another body aboard a gurney being hauled.

Once his driver is paid, he sends a few knocks at the door as its answered directly by Tanner himself who gets straight to business in the informing after their exchanges in greeting then he's escorted to his lab.

- What's so important that you can't tell me over the phone. What we dealing with, a virus ?

- I don't think so. A virus is a agent that reproduces in living cells. In order for it to be transmitted a person has to exchange bodily fluids. This here doesn't register to any of those perimeters at all.

- So it isn't a virus, it's not a infection, and isn't even contagious. What is it then ?

- I said the same exact thing, so then I started doing my homework on each and every case that's been publicized since it sprung. And I found out that all of them. Each and every situation before it turned violent always involved two people. The person who did the inflicting and the other who obtained the infliction.

- Go on.

- Like take the one in Texas right. It says clearly right here bright as day that man came in and had been applying for what.

- A bank loan.

- Exactly, it's says during the entire visit things didn't become turmoil until he was given news.

- The bank denied him his loan.

- The same in Los Angeles with the construction worker, it was just him and his supervisor. It was said the worker never did anything until it became clear that his superior called out to another worker nearby. You know why ? Right

- He wanted a new person to fulfill his task or maybe their opinion of his work.

- New York, witnesses accounted that the guard was the most experienced in the entire building. Her actions come at a shock. Things got aggressive once her supervisor as well voiced a comment that potentially led her to her fatality.

- She criticized her work.

- I followed the trail and the same thing happened not only those three instances, but here with the cop, in Chicago with the students, Pennsylvania with the inmate, Virginia, Georgia, Tennessee, and etc. It's not a illness. It's a condition. In our brain the hypothalamus is point that controls man's behavioral autonomy, it governs our function in sex, temperature, sleep, and...

- Moods.

- All these cases we're dealing with, each suspect has been experiencing hypothalamus deficiency. The area in region has decreased or nearly has in a enormous rate. It ultimately led me into entitling it as " DEPRI-enteritis ".

- DEPRI-enteritis !

- Yea imagine a person being deprived of its normal reaction as a human for such a extensive time based on how their viewed from a society standpoint. Whether race, class, or religion. Subjected to this treatment so bombarded that your normal human function dissolves and it creates erratic and chaotic behavior. Just what we're experiencing nationally right at this moment.

- So your saying these people have been corrupted by some random conduct based on having suffering from some prolonging issue regarding race, class, or religion.

- If your skeptical, your the investigator. What is the significant ethnicity as doers in this case ?

- Black.

- And primary receiver to being victimized.

- White.

- So naturally if a person who's been so deprived giving this reasoning and research. What is it to you that can be the cure ? You contradict the treatment of deprivation by trading that behavior that which caused the damage to indulging which now installs a mechanism for...

- ...healing.

Power circles within Davis having now discovered the cure to the outrageous extreme behavioral condition rapidly spreading and soon can for sure at the rate of it's intensity. Finding clarity to himself as he retraces in thought based on his past experiences from the cab ride and airport that the answer was always before him but it is now assured to Tanner's theory. And if people are consistently belittled and disregarded warranted with no respect by authoritative powers than the line known before between regulate and regulated will no longer be in existence.

Spontaneous to the moment a called summons from his phone and he answers it to a calm but twisted liberated in the mood Maher. Who starts things off in great demand wandering where Davis was and how come he hasn't been in touched in the last hours. Calling that things have now reached a devastating point and he expects his appearance right of way. Agreed is from Davis having following his superior orders but luckily in great news on his end he proceeds afterwards in explaining once his arrival is present that he in fact have the solution and cure to their problems during this social crisis.

Maher slows him down before he goes to explaining and suggests he holds off with the revealing until he arrives back at the office at once, there's a new plan being taking into effect. In route Davis assures he is following ending the call. Preparing himself to Maher's office, he thinks a moment and asks Tanner to accompany based on his evidence to which he found and would do more convincing during the explaining.

Maher meanwhile awaiting on Davis's arrival. Arms himself in the meantime with private artillery stashed in a secret compartment within his office. He arms himself along with the rest of soldiers confined in his office. Committing their role to exterminate any and every person that has came down with the speculated infection within the entire city.

External to his orderly sanctuary crept beneath the shadows, place beyond the twilight silence, amongst the trail of gore left behind in bodies lurking in sight at his door panting in and out rests Mercer up in arms loading a new round and then cocking it after in prepare just steady lingering, patiently waiting almost for a open opportune as the voices ascending from Maher's office hovers into the hall.

Knocks slam up against the door that raise a heightened in security taking by Maher and his men inside as they aim straight their weapons in direction rattled in fear. Maher behind his desk before he moves in signals three by his side to fire at the call of his hand gesture as he moves in when again incomes more knocks banging up against the door seeking answer. Stepping softly and cautiously before the door, he places his hand on the door knob signaling again with his hand as he proceeds to unlock as they all assure to follow his command. Open fast he does the door, guns aimed to the outside from all over. Surprise to find it isn't anyone to be unexpected or there in harm but Davis and Tanner who look in alarm reaching their hands in surrender above their heads.

- This is your plan, it's only me.

He says before stepping inside.

When he does Davis enters and one of Maher's soldiers closes it in return like before.

- I thought you was fucking Mercer, you know it got into him. Go ahead back outside that sick son of bitch left a trail of my entire goddamn army out there. This is all my fucking platoon is left to right fucking here, eight men.

- Look Captain I know this thing has exceeded way beyond what you expected and myself. But I'm telling you according to the research that I discovered along with my source here. If you allow me to explain what it exactly is. I'm pretty sure we can take this task and end this without any extreme action taken.

- It's well clear on how to take this fucking problem and solve it.

- But it must be dealt with delicately Captain this isn't what is painted in the media, news, or by analysis. This isn't a disease, virus, or infection. These people aren't senseless zombies out for blood like portrayed. It's more than that. Tanner here found the way. Tell him.

Going over the truth in detail, not leaving out as one clue missing. Tanner explains what their dealing with in regards to the condition and how to neutralize it for good without even the thought of using violent behavior in the midst. Maher hears and his obtaining is expected.

- "DEPRI-enteritis"...so all your saying is all I have to do in order to restore things is to allow these motherfuckers to ascend naturally within boundaries to the world order, is that it. That's what your telling me.

- If you delete all intentions that overrule and dominate those systematically as well as personally this can all be behind us.

Davis prefers strongly.

- Is that right, how long we're talking.

- You allow these people the same freedoms as anyone else I'd say in forty eight hours. I guarantee things a be where they were a few days ago.

Tanner co-signs.

Maher turns to the view outside his desk where he stares out from it as he glares in esteem scene at the nation's capitol as it shines brightest to white as the moon behind the stars. Then on to the streets he sees patrol lights hover every corner he turns his head that's in response to this sudden chaos that has sprang among them and physically caused them to be handicap. No different than the effects would hold from a strike by a venomous snake.

- That's too much of a period to gamble on, and too many lives that may could be jeopardized at this time and I can't take that risk at my position and I wont.

- Now look captain you asked me to do my job and I did. I made good on every task, and now I'm expecting you to do the same. You can't just wait for two fucking days, seriously only two days that we asking for.

Davis cries.

He can cease on his argument, yield on his view, forget about his so called sure fire plan to be executed. It wasn't going to happen, after his speech in determination Maher signaled his men to prepare and rally out blinded by irrelevance to anything said by Davis at that particular moment.

As he and Tanner standby near his desk while they round up their artillery in backup along with more ammo before heading on out pass the door. Something happens, a strange feel comes over Davis first, then Tanner second. Davis standing there alongside Tanner and both face before the view behind his desk. He calls out Maher by name in a heavy tone that can't go unnoticed or ignored this time oppose to captain.

- MAHER...

- Your off the case Davis, your fired, now take your faggot nurse friend home and leave my office the way it was when I'm gone. That's an order.

- ...I forgot one thing.

- What ?

He asks angrily.

One of his men opens the door proceeding to depart but is ferociously unexpectedly met by Mercer breathing in and out like a fire breathing dragon as his uniform is drowned in his fellow soldier's blood during his rampage standing with his M-4 up in arms in combat mode with his finger itching to squeeze the trigger. They all including Maher sees, in the next instance out in hollers racing toward them faster than a snap of a finger maniacally almost possessed goes Davis and Tanner all at once with death and vengeance prone in their eyes as Maher curdle in his womanly screams staring face to face in victim to the attack.

THE END

INTERMISSION

...dozens stand up to claim prize, they touch hands on the round orange ball, reach a perfect firm on it, and then extends it out from the position to where they are as many stare on that uniquely isolates all of the contestants and lookers past the blacktop area and into the confines behind a black gate that surpasses the thirty feet area clearly. And each time they put up a brick that catches near the hoop but fail to sink in goal pass the white shackled net. EVERY, SINGLE, TIME.

How long their duration has been underway is unknown but for sure is the pair gains more richer every time that hoop hits a clank. Then yet another person steps to the throne in claiming but too find themselves digging in pockets to pay and not reaching for their prize. The figure in point of a view a young boy near his teens stands in clear angle before the top of the key behind the gate. Turning his eyes at those who try from all areas in making the hoop whether east or west corners, classic three point range, and of course top of the key. Standing within the large massive crowd and being as one with the countless others who just stand and look on and watch as tons lose out in their money.

Something when in the viewing in every contestants release he notices and it has nothing to do with how they bend their knees, spring upward for pressure in shooting, or the snapping at the wrist when to release. The discovery is a little bit more covert than that although it does intertwine with those important inclusions to the contest.

It just so happens a dude tall enough and if on the blacktop could slam it through for a dunk with no problem decides to try his chances as he passes by innocently with his girlfriend and young daughter. After being heckled almost by the host for a few shouts he's baited in as to playing. The man can no longer resist with all eyes on him and his energy from him feeling just like he's been a collegiate player or a all state star guard at one time. Nevertheless he escapes from his windbreaker for his young daughter to hold before lending these words to her.

- Hold this for your daddy.

Twirls over the ball in a rotation motion like he's at the foul line through his hands for a desired grip about twice before he does it. He hunches over as he bounces the ball, tucks down, springs up, then releases the shot. Smooth sailing the ball goes in direction to all knows where. From what it looks the angle looks dead on as to hearing the golden noise within the game SWOOSH. It lands and the first stop it trickles a few centimeters inside the hoop before a bounce retract sends it in a return into the air oddly as it rolls right in a miss. That's was all she wrote before the pretty girl in the short, shorts had her hand out for that kick back. Coughing up a dub like as she says sorry for his loss and him paying it like it wasn't clearly his last before stepping off. The rotation continues on, the host meddles in search of anyone else looking to get lucky (more like lucky sucka). Finding his way in direction towards the top of the key where the man was and overlooking any potential prospects.

BREACH

A luxury vehicle speeding in hurry, easing on the break, and then sliding into a empty lot space. After exiting and slamming the door behind him. The driver, a well dressed man in a suit and mirrored polished shoes is shown his way through in all access rear exterior door by a female wearing a earpiece. Her demeanor screams anxious in mood and appearance appears busy in a bustle. Calling in direction to the driver as he makes himself her way.

- Here, Mr. Dietrich…yes he's here.

She says communicating with him and through her earpiece.

Hanging by she leaves the door open for the gentleman as he enters in a rush. The door slams close in impact compensating to the loud noise that sort of simmers from speaking that can be heard alongside a possible huge crowd or audience. He's shown through the hall to a door that prints the name in the dead center "Guest Room 1".

Watching live from a flat screen goes the gentleman while hydrating himself with water as a female standing dabs his face in powder for a few minutes then runs over his suit collar and shoulders with a lent roller. When finished she states he's good to go and then she exits the room. To his lonely the man clings further into the television raising the volume to the program housing the host before a live studio audience. As the host a white haired male well beyond his sixties who's too garbed in a suit proceed into his dialogue met with a apologetic disposition.

Removed at this time the gentlemen unleashes his phone from his pocket as he peeps the time unlocking the device, then indulging himself to a message that in some way made its way via text. A few clicks to the screen and he opens it to see the receiver is from his wife. Enclosed the note reads. "Relax, take a deep breath, and do what you came to do. Love You."

The knob on the door turns as the raving applause from the television blares loudly that he doesn't notice as the door opens to the female with the earpiece that escorted him in. Her presence is strict to the informing as he turns over to hear.

- Ten minutes before live, Mr. Dietrich.

She says.

- Thank you !

He nods.

As she goes to shut the door scrambling from individuals in the halls can be seen along with the noise. Passing on the message, she departs immediately after. He responds in good graces to her message and then finishes his water before getting a good look over himself in the mirror. Glancing over his suit, hair, and importantly his facial point. He takes a moment and real hard stares at his reflection locking focus to himself really concentrating almost as if there's something there or maybe wrong.

Settling in comes knocks at the door that's signal for his final preparation warning that snatches him away from his prior exercise. It's time for him to go. Out he goes from the guest room where he's once again escorted to a space behind a stage. Where cameras and several faces including the female with the earpiece dwell operating as hundreds of people can be heard in strange noise gaps. On and then off. One of the faces in the midst happens to be a male, a bit young in age. But still he approaches the gentlemen in good natured.

- Mr. Dietrich I saw you for the first time about four years ago when you spoke at my school.

- Where you'd go ?

- Chaney, you were on a panel about...

- ...urban economic displacement.

- Yea I love the way you broke down unequal disparities between black and white involving loans and gentrification being on the rise. You help me a lot to open my eyes to that fact.

- Thank you, young brother.

- No thank you professor. I know your always going to do the right thing.

- Guaranteed ! Are you the one handling the cameras tonight.

- Yes sir.

- Well do me a favor.

- Anything.

- Just make sure that lens get my black side when I'm out there.

- Sure !

He chuckles as they go to embracing with hands in mutual solidarity.

The host commences before his audience physical and live staring before the cameras beginning to introduce his guest in typical talk show host mode.

- Now my guest for tonight ladies and gentlemen is very special and dear to me. There isn't too many people I consider as a friend and more than anything a person entrenched in the most respect, peace, and inclined to honor like this man is. He's a professor out of NC State University, a highly recommended lecturer and motivational speaker, also well acclaimed in esteem to his scholar career, and as of last year a best selling author. So please would you give a warm and loving welcome to the show Mr. Eric Henry Dietrich.

The crowd swarms in a show of hands for him as he's greeted down next to the host and they get directly into business in a immediate after.

- Now first things first your very presence here today is based on comments that I would admit were minor and elementary to be making and for that I apologize. But to when stating that I in my position have to realize and be careful with the words that I choose especially a word most sensitive to our society but most specifically to a group that the professor does identify with racially. I understand the backlash. I did it, I made a mistake, and I apologize.

- Oh for sure you are and I don't think anyone is questioning that. I think the trouble and uproar comes at your position in making the comment especially making mentions to a guest who is black saying as you said "Look here boy". Is extremely offensive and totally uncalled for.

- In regards to what I said. How did it make you feel when you first heard it come viral and knowing me as your friend and how could this possibly affect our relationship.

- Thinking back and again being completely honest to the situation. When I first became aware of the comment I didn't think you meant it in any harmful regards as it was taken by the majority because I've known you personally for almost ten years and know your true heart being a caucasian man and me being a African american or more popular term that I prefer as "New Black". It seemed almost as a joke.

He says while the crowd join hands in agreement to his statement.

But behind the support there's a settling nerve Dietrich feels after making his comment having looking out to the audience. Discomfort sits in his front lap as the host also agrees in fact to his explanation. The nature of the show has now turn a completely different direction than expected by some.

Once it has ended Dietrich strays to behind the curtains where he's met with his manager who was tardy on set and approves his performance after he asks.

- How'd I do and be honest ?

- You were superb other than that tie. Blue goes on grey nothing other but that's a different story. I love the way you tied in the book to hook and sinker any buyers in closing to push you above two hundred thousand units. Not too early, way too late, right in that breezeway, exquisitely perfect. I'm proud of you, this appearance alone will keep you on the road for the entire year and half. I've already gotten calls for you to make some appearances to speak.

- Where ? Tell me ?

He smiles.

- Ohhh just...Columbia, Cornell, Dartmouth, and Stanford.

- Good news Ivory.

Smiling he says.

Noticing the young camera man waltzing his way he reaches out his hand to shake it upon his departure having the liberty as to meeting him. But something is wrong, instead of receiving a return he only gets a cold shoulder as the youngster just eases by him like he never even saw him. Despite Dietrich catching his eye. Natural reaction is him turning to his manager Ivory knowing he had to have seen.

- First he tell me how much he admired me, then I'm invisible.

- Uh I don't think any parts of your performance tonight could be invisible especially to some.

- What ?

- What you expect ? You played the safe card.

- In English Ivory, what the hell are you talking about.

- Got damn what I have spell it out for you. You know what you did and what you had to do and I promise when all this blows over we're going laugh about it all the way to the bank. Now finish up here I'm going to get the car, I'll be waiting for you in the back when your ready.

The host approaches Dietrich to thank him after the show has ended and for his appearance. Then he whispers in his ear another thanks for considering his show after his comments feeling he thought his career was over but not anymore after his sacrifice. Unknowing to what he means. His only response comes after the promise of whatever he needs in favors at anytime is his. They cling hands in farewell. The only thought he simmers is over his shoulder to the camera man that he was most friendly acquainted with earlier as his back is now toward him in his departure.

Meeting Ivory in the car, he goes over with him to not sweat the pro black public he refers to after his appearance. Stating that what he did is the business and that all the greats have to do it in order to survive maintaining an industry career if plans to eat from the business. Somethings are never personal he refers to.

- You worry too much, at worst your twitter account direct message will be filled with threats. Nothing more. You can't take things like this personal it's all in the role.

- I get it, but earlier I just had a bad feeling. Not the ones from a upset stomach, but more as regret than anything.

- Regret it's good, it's natural. It shows you have a conscience. Everybody goes through it. I did too first starting out. But we all come to terms to things we must do even though they might be things we don't too much care for. It's your rights of passage, I figure you should know this by now.

- I told you I get it.

- And as far as your stomach goes, only feeling you should be feeling is for hunger. Which is what I want, let's get something to eat.

He says.

A local fast food joint is selected between the both of them. Entering inside they flow into the busy line awaiting like the other customers to be serviced. Wandering over Dietrich becomes curious to something he sees ahead of the line as it lies on what he believes to be a teenager's little old t shirt. There's words on the shirt that for some reason fixate his attention into glaring at the message as it quotes in a definitive structure.

"an infraction or violation, as of a law, trust, faith, or promise."

After reading naturally stirring him into trying to clue himself internally to what could be the term's root word. He tells himself he's worrying too much. So he shakes the paranoia and turns his thought pattern into another direction.

- It's May, just one more month left.

Dietrich words.

- Your gonna drive me up in a fucking heart burst more than her. She couldn't stop calling me all day yesterday telling me that she had to have some fucking shoes to match her exact hat and robe. Over and over "Dad, these are the shoes.", "Dad, what do you think ?", "Dad, their on sale here." I nearly turned my phone off on my own daughter. I'm paying nearly a hundred thousand in tuition and now some shoes. Be lucky you have a son.

- Trust me I am. How much we're the shoes ?

- Three seventy-five.

- Do the muthafuckas at least fly out the box.

- They ought to be for that much. Then she got Rochelle all last night to bring it up so she can remind me, knowing I was going to be in the city all day with you today.

- All the hustle...so did you get them or not.

- What you think ?...

Ivory asks positioned behind him in line.

Dietrich looks over his shoulder in his eye confident to him giving into his daughters temptation.

- Say it !

- Four hundred and two dollars, and fifty-three cents. The receipts in the car I'll show you when we get back.

Dietrich laughs momentarily in joking spirits. As the teen with the shirt ahead of him that caught his attention before reveals more of the message encrypted that halts his joyous emotion to now a reflective one that drives his temperature to a more worry as originally. The teen happens to turn from behind and to his front where the word blazes across his chest clear as day beholding the words capitalize "BREACH". Seeing this causes more mystery having seen Dietrich as they move ahead the line are near next to being serviced.

Asking for the time Ivory does with Dietrich as their kept in line making small talk to pass the time quicker. Behind the two, freshly from the outside are two more individuals but more younger in comparison to their age maturity. A woman ahead of Dietrich goes first before him while in line as he's up next. Further into the conversation a sudden noise is heard that sounds of people speaking but more to a video. Pausing hits the two from their conversation immediately having hearing it. They notice the rambling and on their ears its a little familiar and the recognizing becomes even more greater as tune in more.

- What is that ? You hear it ?

Dietrich asks.

- Yea !

Turning around they see one of the younger dudes on a phone device and what appears to be him watching indeed a video yet on a phone. Ivory identifies the sound in perfection and calls it to be in fact Dietrich. It's not only him but it's his latest interview he sees from the talk show he just got finished appearing on after the taping not too long ago freakishly odd.

- That's you ?

- Yea it is. How'd they get that out so fast ?

He asks.

When its clear it's him the two dudes lock at each other before one confirms once again when he asks.

- This you...in the interview ?

The unknown youngster asks.

- Not me, but my client.

As Dietrich attempts to wave to the young brothers in friendliness. The woman ahead finishes her order and moves aside while the cashier calls for the next customer. Ivory sees and shoves Dietrich to approach the counter as the next moments go in race to the unforeseen. In seconds having putting away his phone the youngster pulls a metal razor that's small as bottle cap tucked from within the cheek of his mouth. Ivory closest with his back turn feels a slight hand on his shoulder pulling him back and as he turns a slice to his lower right jaw that opens him up so fast he never knows what happens except to clinch his hands to his jaw. Before everything can register another slice from the youngster swings this time splitting his hand opening his skin to gush.

Finally noticing goes Dietrich as he feels by instinct Ivory staggering away backwards while the youngster has his way with him in two more slices until he drops to the ground holding himself in his red bodily fluid as the entire restaurant migrate away from the happening to watch. The cashiers retract from the registers in fright as the screams carry on behind the ongoing assault turning deadly before their eyes.

Cornered now by the two young men Dietrich is as he begins to back peddle pleading for them not to hurt him. Before he knows it he stumbles over Ivory cradled there on the floor rattling in shock by the cuts. In a quick turn as he looks to his suffering manager there on the floor and back to his opponents. A slice he feels knits his ear and face that rushes to pour in blood that intensely spills from his hand before Samaritan's standby can take no more before getting involved. Rushing them from behind both the youngsters as the second sends a punch to Dietrich causes him to stumble into the wall. As the detaining on the boys ensues it gives a opening for Dietrich in freedom to the restaurants exit after he sees Ivory withering on the ground. Out he bolts through the door and down the block clinching his hand while his wounds bleed profusely down his clothes covering him in red in the public as all walks of life in the street sees.

When he makes it a few paces feeling he's ahead of his assailants stumbling into a few people on the busy Manhattan streets. He sees NYPD at the curb and informs the cop of who he is and the situation as he points behind him in the direction of the restaurant and where he believes he's still followed. But there's nothing there, even people on the street seem to be removed in sympathy as if they don't even see his injured disposition.

The cop sees and becomes weary of Dietrich moving him away from his cruiser mindful of the blood while he continues to call for the cop to help him on account to his rapid blood loss.

- Who did this to you ? Can you tell me their names ?

The cop asks.

- No, please help me !

Exhausting cries.

- Where did this happen ? Do you know ?

The cop demands.

- No, please help me !

Again he says in exhausting cries.

- Ok, don't move, stay where you are, and turn around.

The cops informs him while removing his handcuffs.

As he places one on Dietrich wrists his head begins to spin as he pictures a large mass of people including the two youngsters who assaulted him and Ivory surrounding around the car staring at him in shame before he collapses to the ground having being overwhelmed by the attention. When his eyes awake to consciousness, still bound within this nervous trance surrounded by these people only this time he's on the ground. Looking above as they stare down at him without expression. He does the only thing he knows how to do in the discomfort.

- Someone please help me.

He cries in weakness.

Remaining there in a group gaze does the crowd until a pocket opens amongst them and emerging to the forefront is the youngster vicious with his trusty blade with his friend to accompany at his side gleaming despise as the others. Then him flashing a pistol there before Dietrich's face as he shrieks in hysteria crying calling repeatedly "no" before the trigger pulls and blasts awakening him to his true state as he gasps alive to find himself bedridden in a hospital. Feeling to his face he nudges fingers to his cheek finding it bandaged. Racing to a mirror from the bed he goes to gently peel away the bandages from his face for a peek at how serious his wound is on his face that perhaps could leave a scar for eternity.

The damage is more severe than he expected as Dietrich the coward he is, can only venture the cut splitting into the side of his face then glimpses it entering in the area near his ear as he endures the excruciating pain having seen the wound and his stitching. Tragic emotions racing him having to been opened up the way he was, questions internal as to why him. But his pondering in deep agony is intercepted as a voice at the door becomes is heard in reference to him.

- Over a hundred stitches...

Quick in turn goes Dietrich over at the door where he sees a man in a white gown that fears him to step away back towards his bed in panic.

- Who are you and why are you in here ? If you come any closer I'll kill you.

He says.

- ...please don't worry, calm down your excited in fear it's quite normal and understandable. I'm the doctor that did the repair on your face.

Consuming his inform right away after his reveal, it immediately settles Dietrich fright as he sits down back at his bed as the doctor moves in closer while explaining.

- I have to get out of here, right now this minute and get home. I have meetings to attend, how long will this take to heal.

- You'll see results in six weeks or more so, if your allocated time to heal. As far as your meetings go ? If I were you I wouldn't jeopardize my appearance going out anywhere.

- That bad of a scar left doc, we'll don't worry about me. People like me have enough to complement a big after the surgeon is finished.

He says racing putting on his clothes carefully.

- I know who you are, also what you did ?

- Who doesn't ?

- If no one didn't know you by now they most certainly won't after. Do you know your manager was killed.

- What did you say ?

He says halting in his racing to his applying his clothes.

- Ivory Jordan, age forty-eight according to my documents slashed severely almost as bad as you, expired in ambulance upon arrival here. I don't think you realize the extinct to what it is your mixed up in. The extreme repercussions from your actions that has caused this savage act to taking place out in the open like it was.

- What are you saying ? What repercussions ? What fucking actions your insinuating ?

He cries out aloud within the room.

The doctor pulls from his pocket a remote and aims it to the room television in the corner and on it comes showing his appearance on the show and his rhetoric used. Dietrich sees.

- This is why your in what is known as a "Breach"…don't worry you aren't the first or the last to have the experience…but your chances in maintaining survival are not even close to happy ending. Many like you I've known have suffer the same fate. Only there's aren't announced as is once they fall.

- Wait what the hell is a "Breach" ? How did you get it ?

- Let's just say it's unwritten rule coded by certain individuals of the public world that I assume you have no knowledge of which makes no sense when you say you stand and speak for all black people. Obtaining it comes from someone of the likes of you, how can I say this " when saying things against the community and the ethnic background to which he belongs aligned with the system". This show you appeared on and what you said makes you now culpable to the perimeters of that violation and it cannot only affect you, but as well as anyone that you love including members of your family. This is why I say do you not understand because what happened to you, what happened to your manager isn't going to stop until you make right, the wrong you said on that program with the likes of that host.

- And how do I do that doc ? I guess I have to pay every nigga for what I choose to say, is that right.

- People underestimate the powers and the stimulating effect an a apology can bring.

Ignoring his comment, racing to his phone with the screen and shield all over it covered in smears of blood Dietrich goes to dialing his phone for his wife. When she answers he hears a long mess of arguing cries for his presence stating that she was told he was dead that also proceeded with a wide range of death threats that not only singled him out but herself and son. The doctor looks on still at his side.

Further detailing on the subject to their son that he's in trouble and that he needs to return home quickly. To which he assures in dear sincerity before trembling in pained worriment ending the call. He demands a favor from the doctor to the emergency of his situation.

- I need to get out of here and more than anything I need a ride home to my wife and son RIGHT NOW. Can you help me ?

- You didn't hear what I explained to you, your under "Breach" grounds now. My participation or anyone for that matter in assisting you now and anyway makes you accessory. The rules in place are no different than american law except punishment results in you being inducting under the breach as well. Sorry I can't help you, my very converse with you at this moment is enough to put me in violation.

Dietrich shields his chest with his shirt and suit jacket, angrily gather the rest of his belongings and then his shoes charging to the room's threshold in exit before furiously shoving over a room tray on account to his frustration of the doctor investing otherwise as to not lending his assistance. He leaves a few words to him before he's out, the doctor does the same.

- Thanks a lot for all your help. Can you at least tell me how the hell to get out of this place.

Sarcastically he tells.

- Mr. Dietrich...James Baldwin quoted once "People pay for what they do" remember that. The elevator is out the door, down the hall, and to the left.

He responds.

Dietrich ascends through the hall in a hurry, navigating the directions like the doctor informed him and it isn't too soon he starts to notice many patients, visitors, hospital staff as well all alike him ethnically beaming their eyes his way as he shuffles in movement. The stares of discomfort only give him more pep in his step towards the elevators knowing what roams many of their minds. Passing by seated in the hall as his face is shielded by a newspaper. A man discards it away from his view when it's known upon witnessing as Dietrich flows by him.

Neatly arranging the papers back into its original fold then placing the paper within the seat he sat in as he stands to his feet he proceeds in the same direction in normal. Peeping around anxious in his fast steps remaining mobile in forward to the elevator. In his sprint the man only walks in these very same trails of Dietrich. Glimpsing back the two lock eyes. Before long having came across the elevators and pressing the service button to arrive on his floor, he sees the man again now on his tail and automatically assumes he's being followed. Racing and pushing that button as hard as could seeing and hoping that it'll shoot in picking him up any quicker. Before the man makes over to him out he flashes a gun from his vantage point, open comes the elevator door while income rounds that just nearly misses Dietrich by an inch and seconds and tucks to enter without being touched.

On the elevator grasping for every air he possibly could, he presses for the first floor repeatedly until he's on the ground. When the door opens alive comes more shots aimed in his direction that sends him once again tucking down to his knees in method to not being hit. His advantage comes racing toward the shooter in tackle knocking him to the floor behind a mass body of people who look on in blind fear of what just occurred. Jetting without any look back determined to not be a casualty in his breaching, out the exit Dietrich sees the most unusual that holds almost as familiarity he by a man in a blue uniform, badge, and hat who plays neutral in the shooting.

Outside he looks around in desperate panic while inside the shooter gets to his feet when a new elevator arrives down and the man upstairs assists the one downstairs to his feet locking shots out the door the blast through the glass and gains Dietrich alertness shielding to not be hit. They pursue in jog toward the door while the cursed scholar catches a man entering his vehicle that he commandeers in stronghold that lends him an escape from the hell hole hospital. Tardy in having pleasurable sights on him for his much wanted demise unfortunately their only left with the gleaming red break lights glowing farther and farther apart from them in getaway. So far a bullet could only pray to touch Dietrich but it doesn't stop them from trying at all dumping every bullet they can his way as he skirts off out the lot to his extremely lucky safety.

Arriving home out the car, inches away from his house from the window he peeps in glance at a figure, it's his neighbor a older white widow, Mrs. De'Ville who spies his steps for a moment as he bolts inside having losing interest. She must be on her patrol as usual he suspects with him and his family being the only black resident within the area. It wasn't just a mere three years ago having just bought the property and she phoning in a mysterious call in the late hours into the night to the authorities as he moved in trinkets which led to him being arrested under suspicion even when the property he had just bought was his house. It was claimed to be a mistake and all forgiven on his part and hers too but yet every once in a while parking in his driveway he catches her irritable stare out the window at him. Separate in feelings as to caring, one side partially knowing why as the other doesn't.

Passed the door with his key he calls out for everyone as his wife signals to the kitchen where they embrace but his son stays with his back turned almost ashamed or removed to hug his father. Dietrich turns him around anyway while his wife urges him to don't but it's too late he sees it. His son sporting a shiner that's black, blue, and purple. Then a busted lip also to match it, there in the kitchen his wife began to nurse it with their first aid kit. Pained to the sight mourning his son. The only explanation and the natural one he asks is.

- Who did this ?

- You did ?

His son says.

- Some boys heard about your interview and they cornered him after class.

His wife informs in whisper to him.

- It's your fault, none of this would of happened if you never would said the stuff you said. Now we have to suffer. I HATE YOU !!!

His son yells before launching off past him to his room upstairs. Employing that he don't go after him his wife suggests in feel that he may need to blow off some steam and that he'll feel better later when the situation calms. Feeling different now knowing what he knows. He asks his wife something very important before looking her in the eye.

- Are you alright ?

- Yes. Are you ? What happened ?

She says minor hesitantly.

- Never mind that. Are you sure ?

- Yes.

She says again hesitantly.

- I have to ask you something and listen carefully because it's extremely important and our lives may depend on it.

- Your scaring me Eric. What is it ? And what's going on ? What the hell is going on ?

- This is going sound ridiculously silly. But have you ever heard of a such thing as a "Breach".

He says while wandering the house, perhaps in search for something.

- A "Breach" no I haven't, does is have something to do with what you said. What are you looking for Eric ?

She says in panic as he races up the stairs to their room.

- Eric...Eric...

She calls out aloud coming up the stairs. Then entering the room.

To where she uncovers him armed with a revolver sinking bullets into each chamber.

- What are you doing with that Eric ? And what the hell is going on ?

She cries as the bedroom television replays his quotes from the interview that he sees.

- There was this doctor at the hospital see, and he tells me that I'm under something called a "Breach". Because of what I said on the show. People, black people are taking offense and now looking to collect vengeance with our lives the way he put it...a kid slashed my face in a McDonalds while I was with Ivory, he ended up getting it the worst. After talking to you, a man then followed me and nearly shot me to death inside the hospital in front of everyone. People just sat by and played as if nothing was going on.

- What ? Where's Ivory ?

- He's dead...the doctor told me. I didn't believe him but in the moment I did. It's confusing, I don't know ?

- Call him and find out, right now.

His wife pleads.

Instantly the phone rings and blares throughout the house, it doesn't get a chance before Dietrich snatches it from the charger and answers finding it to be a hostile voice on the other side.

- Hello ?

- ...you muthafucka, it was you, you did this.

- Ebony please at least hear me out.

He recognizes.

- I don't want hear anything. Ivory is dead. I just got the fucking call from the hospital you son of bitch. When were you going to tell me ?

- Too much has happened ?

- Really ? Too much has happened so I have to hear from two piece of shit cops that my husband, your manager. Was sliced to death in a restaurant defending you. They said he had multiple razor wounds that were inches long on his face and torso. He sat there and bled to death while you ran away and left him. And all because of your coonin'...but you know what I have a little surprise for you. Because there's something else I was told, and it was you was under a "Breach". And being that you felt too much was happening as to not informing me about my husband's death. I felt the need in waiting on your death would be too much for me and everyone else. So I felt the liberation in submitting your address live on twitter. That should make everything even, I think.

- What ? What the fuck are you doing ?

- What needs to be done. Now you and your family can see what it's like to be vulnerable to death. Log in you can see how many likes and responses I've gotten in the last forty-five minutes.

- You bitch ?

- Tell your wife it was nice knowing her.

Phone disconnects.

His wife alongside him asks in frenzy what occurred between them during the phone call, what words were exchanged as she feels the temperature. He never replies only skimming his Twitter to where he finds Ivory's wife page and there it is before the screen as he looks directly at it.

- Oh my god ! Why did she do this to me ?

- Who Ebony ? What did she do ?

She asks.

He reveals the post after explaining as she erupts hysterical to seeing. Then goes her eyes trickling down to the countless replies that vow to emerge at their home with deadliest intentions. Many state in clear that they're coming to not only to execute Dietrich but everyone within that house. Incredible amount of fright stimulates his wife all over demanding that they all evacuate the house.

- We have to leave now, we have to go.

She cries. Calling out to her son in his room steps away.

- What you don't understand, WE CANNOT GO ANYWHERE. Outside are people and if this shit is as real as said those people will KILL US. We're on our own, we have to stick together now. Let me make a call to the host, he said if I ever needed anything he'd help me. Maybe he could fix this, so just hold on.

He roughly suggests as he unveils his phone.

Secluded to his room goes their son Gregory who's one with his privacy alone. Stretching his eyes in distaste but unresentful to the negative bash he receives on social media from school classmates and friends. Reaching beyond disrespect that a laughing stock would endure and even below the likes to a geek could be picked on for. The comments don't stop at all as his Twitter inbox incomes a new direct message one after the other targeting him with a variety of nasty names on account to the breaching and his father's unforgivable comments made in against the race on the show.

"BITCH-ASS SON OF A TRAITOR", "PUNK ASS FATHER", "DEATH TO ALL COON ASS NIGGAS LIKE ERIC HENRY DIETRICH", "TELL YO FATHER HIS ASS GOT DAYS ON IT".

The range of insults went on and on to the point Gregory could no longer tolerate it, so he just shut it off, his account, his phone, everything altogether where the only thing left is him inside his room anger to the point he wants to weep in shame lying there on his bed.

Suddenly he hears a noise outside at his window that for something strange lends to his attention. Moving closer to the window he can only try to remember what the noise sounded like before opening it. Just as he does, there it goes again. It rhythms to a small object, like a stick or a tiny pebble knocking up against glass. When he raises the window in suspicion after the second time, he glares with his head poking out the window looking first to his left, then right, and last to the ground that wasn't too far down but a define view.

There was nothing there, bringing his head back in he stares from without his window's scenery once again before he shuts it. In stride back to his bed, there it goes again twice at the same time. Forging him back to the window out of annoyance as he yells in outburst poking nearly half his body out to look around again. When he does up above in a split second goes a person in a face mask with a blue shirt who latches on to the boys neck tightly that he launches him from the window in soar for a moment with only a crack in scream can be heard until his body hits the ground where it lays there awkwardly behind a thud. The only thing left in his room goes the breeze wind after the fall and one of his sneakers that didn't make the trip inside near the window.

Dialing the number as it rings goes Dietrich to the host of the show. Instantly a nerve strikes his wife and she ventures to their son's room door calling for his state in mood.

- Gregory, baby are you alright ?

She says into the door. But he never responds.

- I know your upset and angry about what happened but I need you to open the door it's important.

She calls. But again, no response.

Expeditiously into a panic twisting the door knob each way hoping for a opening but unsuccessful in her attempts. Downstairs to the kitchen she descends while Dietrich aims for assistance during his call desperately with the host.

- This is Bill.

- Bill it's me Eric.

- Eric...who ?

- Eric Henry Dietrich, I was on the show this morning.

- Oh that's right ! I was just mentioning you to some friends on behalf to the show by the way congratulations on the attention from the interview, my assistant said you killed. I have to have you on again. When is the next time your free ?

- That's not what I called you about Bill, I can't tell you if I'll ever be on the show again. Because I may not even be alive that long enough, I need your help right now...it's urgent.

- What do you mean ? Is this about your breach ?

- How do you know ? Yes it is...

- And you want to know if I can't help you, right.

- Yes that's exactly it, can you ?

- Sure I can, no problem...

Overjoyed he is having to hear him agree at his time of fateful need. Dietrich listens on further as he supposedly alludes to how he will be of assistance.

- ...but will I ? No.

- What the fuck you talking about early today you said if I need any help with anything call you. I had no problem helping you for what you did last week on account of today.

- Yea see here's the thing, I tend to say things that intentionally I don't really mean especially with the likes as someone like you.

- You muthafucka you fucked me, you did this to me.

- You learned negroes kill me, your all the same. You hate your kind just as much and maybe even more than we do and think your anything more than different. I didn't say no on account of you being a nigger. I said no because even though I'm white doesn't mean I get involve with "breaches". If I saw what they did to you, who do you think is next. That's too much of a mess for my invitation, but for what its worth. I really appreciate what you did today. Everyone is in uproar to what you said, that my stupidity isn't even in question anymore. I would invite you back but...oh yea, that's right...well it was a pleasure. And oh yea, give your wife my love.

The conversation ends.

His wife opening a kitchen drawer clings her hands around a knife and then sprint back to their son's room where she forcibly invites herself in as the door gives way to the inside. She looks around and find no sign of him except only the breeze from the outside his window that's wide open whirling his curtains she notices. Moving closer she sees it weirdly ruffled along with the entire view of the window as it sits unusually wide as it is. She looks down and finds his shoe and more. There's a trail of scuff markings appearing upward on the wall. As she stands she sees it trails outside the window. Dropping the shoe to the floor she lunges her head outside the window and what she sees next can send any mother in a world of curdled screams and never-ending tears.

She calls out his name that it blares the whole block and further had to have heard her. In their bedroom after the call clutching his gun hearing her screams Dietrich runs to his son's room pointing his piece ready and fully willing to drop anything in his sight. It isn't until he lays eyes on his wife screaming and moaning uncontrollably calling their son's name repeatedly as he cradles her demanding she tells him what's wrong feeling to glimpse outside the window seal before.

- What, what, what's wrong ? Where's Greg ?

He asks as she can do nothing but cry and cry more and more pointing to the outside of the window. When he steps to the window not ready for what's over as his wife drops to the floor once out of his arms shedding wet tears down her eyes in a big fit. Dietrich moves close in fear dreading the agony he knows in seconds is about to haunt him. So he doesn't poke his head out of the window but he does steps near peaking out and sees the view of his twelve year old boy lay face first disfigured outside his window.

Emotion or words have no describing in a situation as that one that jerks his body and causes a bit of disillusion having to living the moment in seeing his son murdered before his eyes near side his wife. She moves to her feet struggling while calling in a weeping dialect.

- I have to go cover him up. I have to go cover up my baby.

Dietrich follows her as she exits out the back door with a coat and props it over his young body while Dietrich curses himself looking in pain as to holding himself responsible. That's when a phone call incomes and Dietrich answers while his wife cries over there dead son's body in the grassy yard beyond a forest past their gated fence.

A voice from the call is creepy and deep as it delivers a cryptic message over to just the person who answered.

" Our work ain't done yet, outside, over there in the yard, by his body. "

It says before Dietrich shatters the phone on the floor racing to the back towards the door where he meets his wife trying to flow past him racing.

- I need to put some flowers on his body.

At the threshold he gets a peek to the outside above their gate and looks out not too far within the forest where he counts two figures bearing masks on their faces approaching slowly from the woods and the last to his left shinning a red beam in direction their way that impulses Dietrich to latching on to his wife. He swings her and himself away from the back door and down on the ground where incomes two shots blasting in rapid fire BAM ! BAM ! Catapulting in their direction fiercely lodging in the door's wooden seal, inches away from his wife head, and it being a blessing she dropped in time.

Dietrich right of way closes the door. While lunging back in cries forward to wanting to be with her son after the shots Dietrich grabs hold of her tight and shoves her to the living room while screaming for her to stay down before any more bullets are let loose into the house.

Outside forming as a unit goes the three intruders flowing from outside the yard and near the house all shielded by face with black ski masks. Muted from speaking however they interact with body language. The one closest to the back door schemes eyes over in his direction slowly. While the other signals his eyes with the other to around the house. The last in the middle looks on as his associates take their place while he's left alone shooting his head above the window of Gregory's room where he stands.

When they make way into the kitchen Dietrich's wife explodes into a fit swinging her small tightly crumbled fist in his direction hitting him with as much might she can secure to send a punch back. Cursing him for all that has happened and now with their son lying dead in the yard outside.

- This is all your fucking fault Eric, look what the fuck you did. I fucking hate you, I fucking hate you.

Her shots come consistent even though they roll over weakly on him as he puts a end to them clamoring his hands on both of her arms in stopping her. Shaking her in overwhelm until she draws out her fit some.

- I'm calling the police.

- Your not calling no damn body. You heard what I said the first time. We're not going anywhere and nobody's coming through that damn door.

- Your son is dead Eric, OUR FUCKING SON IS DEAD RIGHT NOW LYING IN THE FUCKING GRASS.

- I KNOW MY FUCKING SON IS DEAD, I SAW HIM JUST LIKE YOU DID. YOU THINK I ASKED FOR THIS, I DIDN'T ASK FOR ALL OF THIS SHIT. I didn't.

- Yes you did, your mind was made up when you went up to that show this morning and now look where the fuck we are.

-Oh so your willing to say this shit now and not before I went on when you damn their coached me just like everyone else before the curtains went up.

-Don't fucking blame me for what you made up in your mind in doing. You wanted to tap dance for racism that's your decision not mines or Gregory.

-Yea well tap dancing sure enough put them fucking clothes on your back, that car in you got in the driveway, this big ass house you can't stop buying shit for with my money that yes I do whatever it is I have to in order to get where I'm going.

-Look at what the results left your son. Look what it's doing to us.

- Where's my gun ?

He says as he allows for that deep statement to sink in.

Up he jumps to look around, in flight up the stairs he goes to search. First he rushes to their bedroom where he last remember having it, but unsuccessful to him there's no gun in his sight. Interesting more than the weapons disappearance Dietrich finds things a little out of place than again he remembers. The closet wide, and clothes scrambled on the floor. It catches his attention then he steps out into the hall where he doesn't sees his wife anymore that sends him in a bizarre feeling having to call out at her by name tracking steps near his son's room.

His wife hears his calls while huddled in the dining room whispering on the phone to the 911 operator the address. Unbeknownst to her as she's stalked from one of a the intruders having to trail that part of the house moving every step along with her remaining unseen. As she shifts back into the kitchen looking to the stairs while the masked prowler allows himself in brilliantly upon her non-detecting. Hoping that she isn't found by Dietrich before the dispatcher alerts her to be mindful of a patrolman in route to her destination and the phone call ends.

Upstairs in his son's room Dietrich calls his wife name once again although she doesn't return a response as he surfs his eyes with his back turn to the door looking over his son's room for the gun with a overpowering feeling nerving him suddenly. Even to the outside of his window hoping to spot any of the intruders, but there's nothing he apprehends that even comes close. Again as he stands continuing to his stares from the window directly about to turn as he calls out to his wife by name again before and when she answers, he turns, Gregory's room door closes as a intruder pops up in surprise from behind raising up Dietrich's own gun and firing up a shot enough to send him out the room the same way his son was.

But it doesn't, the intruder must've been too excited and pointed wrong when he aimed because the shot surpasses Dietrich and gives him room afterwards seeing it pass through the wall to rushing full speed at the attacker knocking away his gun to under the bed.

In cruise on his route goes a officer who gets the alert from the dispatcher to the address of the Dietrich's home and he who turns around in directions to the home full speed on the street, enabling his lights to ensemble with the sirens

In his son's room Dietrich and the intruder begin to roughing one another up in the room as the noise sounds to the downstairs as his wife hears the commotion rushing to the stairs as she opens up the door to find her husband and what looks to be a unidentified man bearing a mask over his face competing in gain over each other in a game that determines strength. Dietrich's on top of the intruder, his hands clinging around his neck. While the attacker does the opposite to him. Managing enough strength he calls out to his wife for help.

- My gun...get my gun under the bed.

Straining while talking as hands grip his neck.

Hearing what he said and near the point to reacting something pulls her to turn around where there's a view to the door. Seeing those two lights flashing red and blue colors is her breath of fresh air to discard her husband's life threatening commands shooting down the stairs, leaving him there as he enrages and punches the attacker a few times before he gives in to surrender. When he does it allows Dietrich in follow to his wife down the stairs while the intruder remains there on the floor in the room appearing totally unconscious.

Outside. Ejecting himself out of the car driving in press focus almost robotic, closing it from behind him as he makes way to the door from behind his cruiser goes the officer.

Inside. Pass the stairs with her touching the knob to open, Dietrich in the middle yelling defiantly for her to resist and don't. Turning at him in disgust and refusing his demands as to opening the door anyways before she can take a step to the outside as Dietrich shouts as loud as he can descending down the stairs.

- NO, NO, NO, NO. DON'T DO THAT !!!

His wife meets eyes with the cop stern in appearance with his service pistol drawn for fire on the steps before their door in exact angle. She doesn't even get the chance to notice his preparing stance is resistance not empathetic to shoot before it happens. BOOM, BOOM, BOOM, BOOM !!! Four shots hit her at the door Dietrich looks on and watches as her body drops, dead on sight. Stepping from the stairs seeing it automatically drops him to the floor, both knees reflecting as if his world is no more as he knows it.

Her eyes poke out at him there at the door dead on her back facing him parallel when the officer approaches, first his shadow over her body as he steps over it, Dietrich's eyes turns from his deceased wife to the cop from foot, to legs, then his piece sticking out from his hands deadly. He no longer stalks, he's at ease in steps moving toward him. The moment is his with his gun in his hand aimed at Dietrich locking in a stare that's mutual but on opposites.

One man the aggressor, the other on the verge to being the persecuted. At his knees and still not accepting to his actions as he plea.

- There's nothing I can say that will rearrange this moment. But let me ask this one question before you do what you came to do. You kill my son, my wife, and me, for what ?... because of what I chose to say on a program.

Dietrich asks on his knees.

The officer at the break of replying looks above the professor to his stairs where the intruder he scuffled with in the room now is armed with his gun, creeps down the stairs. While two others that accompanied merge from opposites sides of the house in reveal. To side by the cop, where they also aim there guns in Dietrich's mug. Before the lead intruder reveals his face announcing himself in identity as the cameraman at the show he met. This stuns Dietrich who's at a loss of words but his expression alone draws himself in surprise before the cop gives rebuttal to his statement.

- You still don't get it do you.

He says.

- And he never will, a people are only as strong as their respect within a structure. Especially in a structure that resents them. About the only thing they do possess is they're respect, they're regard. See in a "Breach" there's no empathizing for those most closest to you. Your treachery to your kind is the stake you chose to put on the table and now it's came to be collected.

Camera explains.

- What about amnesty, resolve, forgiveness. I'm apologetic, look if you want me to say sorry, ok, ok I'm sorry. I apologize.

- You want forgiveness ?

Cameraman asks

- Yes.

- Seek it with your family...with your life...and your decisions like you said you chose.

Dietrich cowardly squirms as he goes to cover his face before all four guns empty rounds in him just before his thought as to sincere regret.

THE END.

EPILOGUE

- You...you...how about you man.

He suggests handing out the ball to entice the audience of onlookers that ends in only decline.

Surfing the crowd leaning with both arms over the gate the host holds the ball before the young boy's face in signal for him to give it a shot. Raising his head slowly, while abandoning arms from the gate to motion he's incline to the offer as he puts hands on the ball. The host responds typical as if he's got another one with the crowd's eyes now burning down on the boy as before it was above him.

- Aite ya'll we got another one, this time he's a little smaller than usual but we can't discriminate the little people on a big man's game. Show little dude some love for his courage. He knows the rules, right ?

The young boy proceeds to bouncing the ball over and over for a minute staring first at the hoop then secondary to the inner blacktop where he sees its just the host and the hostess before moving positions. Away from top of the key, bouncing the ball all the way to east of the gate. A specific place because it houses the gate's opening to which he enters at his own free will with it being unsecured. His move strikes the host immediately.

- Aye shawty you can't come pass that gate. Watch out !

He surges at the boy with the ball in his hand before he jukes him fancy to the floor with a crucial crossover that the host falls for on his way to confront the boy who dares his persistence to the hoop. Getting there with all eyes on him even both hosts. Standing before the rim the boy does the incredible, he lifts the ball and props it at the rim in form of a lay up. Only his lay up on the hoop seems to be removed from the gesture in recompense. Now the ball makes it over the rim. But for some reason have a hard time through. When he comes off the jump he stands there stretching his neck up at the rim like he created his latest creation in art. That wows the crowd that once was embedded in a stir of noise to now shunned silence looking on at what the young boy left behind that cringes the male host to looking away, while the girl is nowhere to be found.

The ball...it just...sits there stuck half way between the rim as the lured in audience stares on at the fix that claimed their attention the entire time.

"In 2017 you can't believe all that you see or hear. Question everything with your own research while you using your given common sense." - Jermar Jerome Smith